# DEFENDERS OF THE WILD

MACARENA SANZ LOZANO
DAVID SANZ LOZANO

To:


Our Friends and Family for constantly supporting us with this project and sticking with us.

# PROLOGUE

Deep within the land, hidden away from prying eyes, lay a castle. But this was not just any castle. This castle stood a mile high, pitch black and towering over the barren wasteland surrounding it. A dark aura surrounded the castle, threatening to never let it leave its grasp. Around the castle monsters littered the arid landscape prowling with blood- red eyes and scarred claws.

However, it was what lurked within the castle that was the real danger. Deep within the walls, beyond the layer of shadows lay a hooded figure, a book at their feet. The figure chanted and cursed, their eyes firmly closed, deep within an evil trance. The wind howled ominously around them as they continued to use the dark magic of the book.

The figure opened their eyes, the hint of a smile at their lips. They rose and glided out of the room making their way through the pitch-black maze of corridors. A wrinkled hand rose from their robe and the door opened.

The person looked up at the pulsating ball of darkness that hung there, kneeling in front of it and bowing their head.

"My lord," the figure began.

"YOU DARE AWAKEN ME?" the darkness growled, the candles flickering uncontrollably as if frightened by its presence. The figure stood their ground as the wind howled stronger and faster and outside lightning struck.

"We have found them at last, " they said loudly and silence filled the room. It stayed there until it was broken by the imprisoned master.

"Where?" it asked, the venom in the tone unmistakable.

"On earth. I shall send a squadron immediately." the hooded figure bowed before the darkness.

"Good. Soon they shall be within my grasp and when they are I will rise again. And nothing, nothing will ever stand in my way again." it said before a low ominous laugh invaded the area, promising destruction, chaos…

And death…

Lots and lots of death…

# CHAPTER 1

# DANIEL

Daniel leaned forward in his chair, his brown eyes focusing on the page in front of him. The maths problems were easy, but he knew he better double check. His hands drummed the table softly while he read through all of his working out. He pushed his curly brown hair back and once again scanned the answers with cunning brown eyes. His fingers moved without purpose, his nervous energy overspilling as he struggled to stay still.

"Times up!" a reedy voice shouted from across the classroom. A short portly man with a pointed white beard (in other words a gnome) shuffled into his line of view and went up, collecting the exams and terrifying the students by assuring them that he did not doubt that they had failed. Behind Daniel, his twin sister, Kyla, was looking nervous. She too had brown hair but instead of it being styled back, it was a mess and she looked stressed. She curled a strand while nervously chewing on her bottom lip; a habit that frequently annoyed their mother.

"Why hello Mr. Whixx, have you finished messing up your chances of remaining in my class?" The teacher sneered. You might think it was weird for an old garden gnome to sneer at you, but the way he did it, made it look natural.

"No sir." Daniel replied, spitting the last word out like an insult which was the only comeback he could think of. The teacher just sneered at him again while turning his attention to his sister. He immediately started looking at her exam, his smile broadening with each page. When he reached the last one, he howled with gleeful laughter. Again, if you thought seeing a gnome cackling to himself was creepy, you hadn't seen anything yet. Kyla started biting her nails while Daniel rose from his seat. He swung his bag over his shoulder and made his way out of the classroom, not worrying about how the exam had gone. He knew Mr. Levy was an irritating old man and the only thing that kept him going was the terror he inflicted on his students.

"Hey, wait up!" a voice shouted from behind. He turned to see Kyla running up to him, piles of books in her hands, her hair bouncing wildly over her shoulders. She fell into step alongside Daniel as he reflected on their life so far. He knew that they didn't belong there. It was obvious from the moment they had started going to school. However, all his mother had told him was that they had once hailed from a faraway world called Ocelia until a great evil had risen and forced them into hiding. Apparently, this had been when they had lost their father and they now lived here.

On earth.

Yay.

Ok, Daniel had to admit that life on Earth wasn't that bad. There were loads of cool stuff and nice people on the street like Rupert the homeless guy whom he usually bought a panini for.

Not a single day went by without Daniel imagining what their life would be like in Ocelia, however their mother was adamant. They could never ever travel there; the dangers were far too extreme.

Also surprise, they were shapeshifters. Which had sounded COOL at first until he found out that people would kill him for that kind of power. Talk about danger.

Daniel kicked a rock up the street as he continued to make his way up the road and towards their house. Next to him his sister skipped alongside him with her nose buried in a book. Daniel fidgeted with some pieces of paper, twisting them in his hands and scrunching them up. As they reached their house, he looked across the neighbourhood. From across the road, he saw a middle-aged man carrying a load of boxes from a moving truck. He wore a navy jumper over some long jogging pants and had a brown beard covering his lower face. He noticed Daniel looking and waved at them, motioning for them to come closer. Daniel and Kyla shrugged and approached the friendly man. He placed his boxes on the ground and rested his scarred hands on his hips. He had an easy-going smile and strong hands which he passed through his hair.

Daniel looked at it bewildered. This man had ginger hair with blond streaks. *What a strange combination.* Daniel thought but before he could think more of it the man introduced himself.

"Hey, could you give me a hand? I'm Icarus, I just moved in and I need some help putting these inside." He spoke gesturing towards the large pile of cardboard boxes which littered the floor.

"Hi. I'm Daniel and this is my sister Kyla." He said, reaching down and grabbing the closest (and unfortunately the biggest) cardboard box. It weighed more than he had thought possible, but he carried it nonetheless, ignoring his sister's amused smile when he almost tripped over the pavement. Kyla shook the man's hand, smiling with that innocent smile of hers and then followed Daniel into Icarus' house, her hands stacked with little boxes.

He pushed the door open with his foot and stepped inside, losing the hold on it and 'accidentally' slamming it in his sister's face. She growled quietly and glared at him, picking up the boxes that had fallen out of her hands and piling them on top of each other.

"Ooops." Daniel gave a small laugh and a shrug then continued towards the stairs and bent down to leave the box, immediately heaving, and flexing his aching arms.

He continued to move boxes into the man's house as his sister continued to glare at him over the pile of boxes in her hands, but he didn't care. They finished with their job, after their final attempt to continue helping Icarus had failed, and opened the front door, leaving Icarus to unpack everything. They moved casually into their own house where their mother was cooking their night's dinner.

"Hey guys, how was school today?" she asked, stirring the pot of stew. Cassie was a very pretty middle-aged woman, who was kind and sincere. She had long blonde hair styled up in a messy-but-striking bun and beautiful aqua blue eyes. In other words, she looked nothing like her twin children. She turned to look at them, smiled and hurriedly turned back to the stew, passing a paper towel over her forehead, which was drenched in sweat.

"Great mom, we had our maths's exam, but you know how our teacher is. Always wants to fail us. He got my paper and started looking through it and..." Kyla stopped midway and Daniel knew that she wanted to tell their mom all about their encounter with Icarus. "Hey, did you see the new guy that just moved in? We were helping him put his boxes in his house."

"No, I haven't seen him." Cassie replied.

"He was nice, but he has a weird style. His hair was all different colours as if he had dyed it wrong. Ginger with blond streaks." Daniel said.

Cassie turned around at once, not at all worried about the steam that the pot had started to give off and more troubled at what her son had just said.

"What do you mean he had streaks in his hair?" Was it just Daniel or did he hear a hint of worry in her voice? Did her smile look forced?

"He had some blond hairs in between the ginger. It was cool!" He said and looked over at Kyla who was frowning slightly, her eyes glued to their mom.

"Is there a problem?" She asked Cassie, eyeing her suspiciously. "Why are you nervous?"

Cassie bit her lip then shook her head, her beautiful blond bun bouncing lightly at the action. "Can you set the table?" She asked the twins pointing to the drawer of cutlery and turning back to the stew which had started to smoke.

Daniel shared a look with his sister. He shrugged and begged her to drop it, but she simply rolled her big brown eyes. She was definitely not going to drop it.

"So, mom..." Kyla walked over to their mom and Daniel couldn't quite cover his groan. His sister was so stubborn sometimes. "Is there a problem?"

Daniel turned around. He tried to hide his embarrassment, rummaging through the cutlery, and grabbing three golden spoons, lingering in the furthest corner of the kitchen, hopefully out of sight. He could see his mother shift uncomfortably out of the corner of his eye and couldn't help feeling a bit curious. What wasn't she telling them?

"Of course not!" Their mom replied. Then hurriedly tried to change the subject. "Now if you excuse me, I need to grab some salt."

"You're holding the salt in your hand."

Daniel whipped around and indeed, clasped in her manicured hand was a silver container filled with white crystals. He saw Kyla narrow her eyes and her mom glance at the salt in her hand, her eyes widening ever so slightly.

Daniel tried to meet his sister's eye and tell her to leave their mom alone, but she refused to look at him. She was too busy staring their mom down.

Cassie dropped her eyes to the ground and sighed. "I think we need to have a long conversation."

***

The twins followed their mother through the kitchen door and into the living room. They settled down onto the large yellow sofa, facing their mom who stood pacing around the room.

She stopped.

Looked at them...

Then continued pacing.

When she had done it about a million times, Kyla got up, no longer able to sit still.

"Can you please stop stalling?" She folded her arms over her school uniform.

Cassie had told them to go upstairs and change but they had ignored her not wanting to waste any more time and desperate for information so now they sat there, waiting, and still wearing their school shirt and trousers.

"Well?" Kyla asked impatiently.

"Ok." Cassie said, worrisome lines creeping into her features. "I'll tell you."

Several minutes passed and she still hadn't told them anything, so this time Daniel got up in exasperation.

"Tell us what?"

"The real reason as to why you are in danger."

Kyla's mouth dropped so fast that it must have hurt, and Daniel felt his own jaw collapsing with shock. They had never known why they were in danger since their mum was so protective of them, shielding them from the truth. Whatever had spooked her now was really important.

"You guys are special." Cassie told them and her eyes had a sad spark in them as she looked them in the eye.

"Special how?" The twins asked in unison, and Kyla shot Daniel a look of confusion like she couldn't believe she was anything but normal.

"I don't know," Cassie admitted. "We'll have to wait and see."

"Wait." Daniel held up his hand. "Why would we be in danger then?"

Cassie wrung her hands.

How was she supposed to drop the bombshell that was the truth?

Unfortunately, she didn't have to as a literal bomb soared through the glass window and blasted the house apart...

# CHAPTER 2

# KYLA

The noise of showering glass was inaudible over the whooshing sound of the attack. Instantly after the sound of the explosion came a terrible echo as if it were the anguished cry of the universe and that's when Kyla awoke from where she lay in a crumpled heap.

Her breathing became haggard, heavy as she choked on the ash all around her and coughed herself back to semi consciousness. Every bone in her body ached as she shifted; even some which she hadn't noticed she had, and she lay there, her mind racing with a sudden realisation.

They had been attacked...

She tried to stand up but collapsed on her shaken legs, her nose touching the surface of her bloody arm. Her bloody arm.

Her mind spun at the sight of it and tears leaked around the edges of her eyes as an agonising pain shot up her body. She was hurt...badly.

She took a sharp intake of breath. Where was her mom? Where was Daniel?

Worrisome and desperation fuelled her, and she struggled upright, her blood rushing to her head but she ignored it, shaking it to clear her mind as she scanned the debris of their home searching for her brother, but he was nowhere in sight. Kyla staggered forward clutching her injured side and choosing to disregard the red liquid seeping through her trembling fingers. She had to find her family. No matter what.

"MOM!" She screamed. "DANIEL!"

"MOM!"

"DANIEL!"

Her voice cracked. Rebellious tears streamed down her muddy cheeks, and she shook with heart breaking sobs that echoed in the silent night. Hope of every seeing her family slipped from her and she broke down into a flurry of angry tears.

She would find out who did this and when she did, they would pay.

"Kyla?"

Her head snapped up at the sound of the strained voice. It sounded vaguely familiar, yet she only recognised it when a figure raced towards her.

"HELP! ICARUS HELP!" She shrieked.

Icarus bent down beside her, scanning her with a deep kind of worry. That was when she realised just how bad she must look, scratched everywhere and bleeding.

"Mom. Daniel." Kyla clasped her hand onto his wrist. "DANIEL! MO..."

"Kyla, we need to get you out of here." He interrupted her calmly. He placed a hand over hers and pulled her up making her flinch at the pain.

She shrugged away from him. "DANIEL! MOM!"

Icarus looked at her sadly as he said "Kyla I think they're..."

"DANIEL! MOM!" She repeated, refusing to think of what the deafening silence could mean. It could only mean one thing...

"KYLA!"

She whipped towards the sound, scanning the dusty air.

"KYLA!" A cough followed the shout and Kyla saw a dark shape approaching.

She raced towards it, strangling it with a hug as she broke

into hysterical tears. Relief boiled inside of her and lifted her sunken heart ever so slightly, enough so that her chest relaxed well enough for her to breathe at an -almost- normal level.

Daniel winced and stepped out of the hug. Kyla's sudden rush of happiness vanished when she spotted the dark wells and marks that dripped with blood all around her brother's body. His face was covered in nasty cuts, and she could only imagine the same on her own ashy face. She passed a hand over her sweaty forehead, noticing as she pulled her fingers away that it wasn't sweat that was stuck to her head.

"Where's mom?" Daniel asked, his eyes lingering on her bloody fingers.

"I..."

A pair of hands pushed her to the ground roughly. Icarus sat between her and Daniel, his finger pressed over his mouth, making a clear instruction; to stay quiet. Kyla looked at him in confusion and was about to refuse the nonsense when she heard something strange. Footsteps. But also, and most importantly: voices.

"Stop struggling!" A deep voice demanded from the shadows of the fog and the shuffling of feet grew closer as well as a muffled sound barely audible and untranslatable. Kyla squinted trying to make out the figures.

"This can go the easy way or the hard way." The voice continued and Kyla's hairs stood on end at the sound of it. He had such a deep voice Kyla was sure it was fake just to sound tough.

Laughter echoed around them as the muffled sounds continued.

"Where are they?" The voice threatened, then more muffled grunts continued until a faint rustle hinted at a tear in fabric and another voice spoke.

A familiar voice.

"I can't tell you if I'm gagged, can I?" Cassie spat from the distance. Kyla tensed.

A loud bang blasted from the same direction followed by a groan and the same voice sneering. "You keep that up and I assure you, something much worse will happen to you. Now answer me! Where are they?"

"You see... I don't think I want to."

"WHERE ARE THEY?" The burst of the booming question shook the patches of dirt around Kyla's feet, and she clenched her fists, standing up fast only to be dragged down to the floor once more by Icarus.

She glared at him. "Let me go."

"Are you crazy?"

"They're torturing my mom!" She whispered furiously.

"If you go, all her struggle would be for nothing! I need to get you out of here!"

She shoved at him but he wouldn't budge, which made her angrier.

"I think Icarus is right." Daniel silently whispered, eyes red and puffy from the scene and tears spilling as another BANG echoed in the distance, followed by a moan which made Kyla's mouth turn sour. She stared at him thinking that maybe he was right. But that didn't make sitting around any easier. Their mom was in trouble and they were crouching down, hiding instead of rushing out to help her.

"Kyla, look at me." Icarus ordered, taking her hand and she forced herself to meet his intense grey eyes, which somehow knew what she was thinking. "If you go out there, you will be outnumbered, and we can't risk that. We can't lose you too. Do you understand?"

"I can't just sit here while she..." She couldn't finish the thought.

"You think I find this any easier?"

"WHERE ARE THEY?" The commanding voice thundered.

"She's not going to tell us anything." Another voice

snarled. "Let's take her with us."

"NO!"

The shout shocked the attackers into silence, and it took Kyla a second to realise that she had shouted the word. She clapped her hand over her mouth, but it was too late. They had heard her.

"Time to go!" Icarus yanked her by the hand, dragging her and Daniel away from the oncoming stampede of footsteps and leading them towards the forest, fidgeting with his jacket as they went.

Kyla resisted and stopped just as a blast passed over her head, singing some of her flying hair.

She decided to keep running.

Her legs ached but she forced herself forward as fast as she could go, feeling dirt fly up around her as more blasts echoed in the background. Ears ringing, she turned, grabbing her brother's arm and pushing him in front of her as they sprinted into the bushes, Icarus hot on their heels.

He overtook them, leading the way over fallen logs and muddy terrain landing on the other side of a bush. He dug into his pocket pulling out a square tile which morphed into some sort of gun, which he pointed at the incoming shadows of pursuers. Blue lightning gusts erupted from the end of it and Kyla saw the silhouettes get thrown back. She didn't have time to ask about the weapon as another series of shots broke out, flying all around them.

"Keep running until you reach the cliff." Icarus ordered, taking another shot. The attackers got thrown back.

"What about you?" Daniel asked.

"I'll meet you there. Don't stop running!"

The twins got shoved forward and they rushed through the darkened trees, darting away from the shots as best as they could. Kyla felt a bullet brush her arm and she pulled it into her chest, pressing it against her bleeding hip whilst she held onto her brother. Feeling Daniel's trembling hands in hers fuelled her feet to move faster than before, determined to get him to safety. That's when they saw it.

The cliff.

"KYLA! DANIEL!" A cheetah sprinted towards them, morphing into Icarus as he reached the twins, drips of red splattered on his face. He reached for their hands and stared them in the eyes. "Do you trust me?"

"Yes." Daniel replied, at the same time Kyla screamed "No!" Regardless of their answers, Icarus gripped their hands tugging them forward towards the cliff.

"No, no, no, no, no, no, no ,no , no, no!"

It was too late.

Daniel screamed but Kyla couldn't even muster a squeak as they plummeted towards their deaths.

# CHAPTER 3

# **DANIEL**

Daniel's scream continued as the razor-sharp rocks closed the distance and his very short life flashed before his eyes. He squeezed his eyes shut not wanting his last moments to be so gruesome and waited.

And waited.

And waited some more. Until finally his body landed with a thump, and he lay limp, flat on his face.

Was he dead?

A groan sounded from somewhere close to where he lay, followed by voices he recognised.

"Are you all right?"

"I think so..." A gasp escaped from nearby. "Daniel!"

"He's ok. He'll come around in a minute."

Daniel moaned and ripped his eyes open, only to have to

shut them immediately as a blaring light bore into his brain. He sat up, instantly regretting it as his legs protested loudly and his ribs ached. Broken bones perhaps...

He rubbed his eyes and forced them open, flinching as his eyes adjusted to the sudden light.

"Argh. What happened?" His mind spun and his brain felt fuzzy, but he managed to look up, meeting a pair of brown eyes. Light chocolate with darker rays fanning out around the bottomless pit of an iris. His sister's eyes.

She looked relieved to see him ok, then she reeled on the man a few metres away. "What were you thinking? You could've gotten us killed!"

"I'm experienced. I knew what I was doing, and I had to get you out of there." Icarus reasoned and Kyla frowned knowing that he was right though she didn't look happy about it. Instead of arguing though, she clasped her hand over her hip, which Daniel noticed was bleeding badly.

"Where are we?" She asked, squinting at their surroundings.

"Welcome to Ocelia- your home."

Iridescent rays beamed from above, highlighting the magnificent gifts of mother nature. The fluorescent flowers sprang from the ground, expanding their exotic petals and spreading their scent around them. Beautiful melodies echoed everywhere, enlightening Daniel and making all his worries vanish as he stood, spinning around, eagerly, his eyes widening with the beauty of it all. Birds of all shapes and sizes flew around Kyla, lifting her loose hair and placing their wings against her face, chirping peacefully as she tried but failed to scare them away. One bird pecked at the scratch on her forehead, and she recoiled, wincing from the pain.

"We need to get you medical attention." Icarus lifted her arm over his broad shoulders, and she attempted to get away insisting that she felt fine, but he held onto her.

"You're not fine Kyla. You're badly injured and most certainly in need of several stitches."

"Stitches?" Daniel squeaked, hugging his own scarred arms tight to his chest in a futile effort to hide them from view.

"Yes, and you will need some too and quickly. You have lost too much blood already."

The thought of blood made his mind spin so much that... he fainted.

***

"Hand me the scissors. Not those scissors, those ones. Nope. Nope. Nope. Yes. Nope. Those ones. Yes those." A voice spoke. Icarus' voice. "Was it really that hard?"

"You have a million different scissors, of course I didn't know which ones you wanted!" Another voice snapped back. Kyla's voice. And Daniel jolted awake.

"Whatisgoingon?" He mumbled. His chin felt odd for some reason and when he reached up, he knew why. The tips of his fingers traced the outline of at least 7 stitches, and he retracted them placing his hand on the side of the bed he lay on. It was a simple white bed, in a simple white room, with simple white walls. There was nothing special to it and it looked a bit like a hospital room.

"Are you all right?" Icarus asked him. His ginger hair had more noticeable blond streaks and a pair of magnifying glasses were glued to his suddenly enormously large eyes.

"I think so. What happened?"

"You fainted, that's what happened." Laughed Kyla from somewhere off to the right. A wall of curtains blocked his view, and he could only assume she was changing out of her bloody, messed up clothes.

Daniel's face burned with embarrassment as his mind imagined the worst-case scenarios.

"You fainted too but not because of the blood loss." Icarus added. He turned to Daniel, trying very hard not to laugh. "She saw the needle and fell right into the bedside table".

"Hey! It was a huge needle." She protested and when Daniel cracked up, she insisted that Icarus show him the medical tool.

Daniel gasped. The thing Icarus showed him was not a needle. It was a monstrous beast that would make grown men cry. He felt like fainting again but luckily, he didn't.

"It's not as bad as it looks." Icarus assured him though Daniel wasn't so sure.

"Yes, it is." Kyla whispered and the curtains parted revealing her looking fresh and all cured. She wore a red and black patterned skirt with a white shirt and black boots. Her hair was styled in two perfect braids making the light flecks of brown in her eyes sparkle and the red streaks in her hair stand out.

Wait... red streaks?

"What happened to your hair?" Daniel asked her, shocked.

"The same thing that happened to yours."

Daniel pulled the bedsheets away from himself as he rushed to the corner of the room, where a large full body mirror stood waiting for him. He glanced at his reflection and indeed, his hair had changed. Now mixed with the chocolate brown strands were layers of lime, green that spiked up in random directions. He reached up to touch it.

He loved it!

"They're so cool aren't they?" Kyla smiled. She grabbed a pile of clothes from the bed next to her and threw them at him. "Get changed."

He nodded. The curtains were pulled around him and he started changing into newly cleaned jeans and a grey shirt. The shirt had a rhino logo over the pocket, and he guessed it was some kind of sports team. He finished up, brushing his hair and then messing it up like he always did, remembering how it used to annoy his mom.

His heart shattered as he opened the curtains.

"What's going to happen to mom?" He asked, his voice hoarse with emotion.

Icarus' expression turned serious. Kyla rushed over and hugged her brother.

"I don't know what will happen to Cassie." Icarus admitted with a pained expression. "But I can assure you that I will do everything I can to help".

The intensity in his eyes was enough to convince Daniel

that everything would be ok- even if it was hard to believe. Kyla's jaw was clenched, and Daniel prepared himself for an argument, but she merely nodded her thanks.

Icarus cleared his throat. "In the meantime, get ready."

"For what?" Daniel frowned.

"A good friend of mine is coming to pick you up. School doesn't start for another week, and you need somewhere to stay in the meantime."

"Why can't we stay with you?" Kyla asked but Daniel came up with a better question.

"What do you mean school?"

"To answer your first question..." He told Kyla. "I live in a small flat, as you can see, which would be inconvenient for you and your brother."

So, this is Icarus' flat? Daniel should've guessed.

"And yes." Icarus turned to Daniel. "You will go to school."

He emphasised the word like he would to a six-year-old, which Daniel found insulting. Of course, he knew what a school was - he was thirteen after all.

"Don't we need to fill out an application form?" Kyla asked with a raised eyebrow.

"Usually yes." Icarus informed them. "But whilst you were

both passed out, I quickly called the school and they told me that you were already admitted. Cassie was always so organised."

Was.

Not is.

Daniel pushed the thought out of his mind as Icarus continued explaining.

"Woodford School of Shapeshifting is one of our most prestigious academies which only the best shapeshifters attend." He stopped, noticing Kyla's frown. "You two are obviously a special case since you haven't had the right education but I have a feeling you will do just fine."

"How can you possibly be so sure?" Daniel asked, suddenly feeling uncomfortable. His mother always said they were special but having someone they barely knew tell them so, felt awkward and he felt himself squirm.

"You'll see." Icarus didn't really answer the question, but he went towards the door anyway like he had said everything they needed to know. "You guys coming?"

Kyla nudged Daniel forward and they left the room, following Icarus through the winding corridors and into a living room with, pretty much, white everything. White walls, white floors, white sofas. There was even a white tv hanging on the wall, its screen broadcasting a natural habitat of what looked like a small cat but when Daniel looked closer, he saw that it was bigger than it looked with an elegant purple mane and white patches on its fur.

"What is that?" Kyla asked but before they could get an answer a bell rang around them followed by weird flute sounds which blasted their ear drums.

"Sorry. I really need to fix that doorbell." Icarus said. He lunged forward and opened the front door revealing a man waiting on the other side.

The man in front of Daniel was extremely tall. He had emerald, green eyes and really shiny red hair with small dark basil green streaks gelled to perfection. His face was wrinkle free, but he had to be about 30 years old no less. He reached out and hugged Icarus before turning towards the twins, smiling with a hint of sadness.

"You must be the twins." He said, extending his hand.

"I'm Kyla."

"I'm Daniel."

They shook hands. Daniel felt surprised at the strong grip of the man, but he shook it just as hard though not as hard as his sister, who he could see was trying to shake the man's hand the hardest.

"I'm Julius Reyhan." His eyes sparkled with kindness and Daniel instantly liked him. He could see Kyla narrow her eyes at Julius and knew that she would be harder to please.

"Well, I guess this is goodbye." Icarus turned and shook the twin's hands leaning in, to whisper something to Kyla, whose expression changed into something Daniel couldn't read and then turned determined as she nodded.

"Have you ever gone through a portal?" Julius asked them, taking a small pink bubble out of his pocket. He caught it in his hand then launched it into the garden outside where it sparked an iridescent pink swirl.

The twins shook their heads, looking at each other in amazement. Kyla shrugged at Daniel, stepping forward towards the circle of light.

Just as Daniel stepped into the light, he looked back at Icarus who smiled.

"I'll see you very soon Daniel.".

# CHAPTER 4

# KYLA

Stepping through the beam of rose-coloured light should've been weird considering that it had just been blasted out of a bubble, but the sensation was actually relaxing, as small fizzes of air blew around Kyla in a refreshing 'summery' way. The teleportation only took seconds, but Kyla clung to each mini bubble which escaped around her, wishing that her worries could do the same.

The pink wash cleared after a few moments and a beautiful scenery came into view. Kyla stepped out of the light, her boots crunching on the evergreen pasture they found themselves in.

"Where are we?" Daniel said behind her, and she turned to find him clutching his head and wobbling slightly.

"What's wrong?" Asked Kyla, rushing over to hold him

steady as he stumbled forward. He held onto her a little too much and she bent slightly at his weight on her shoulders. Her brother might be small, but he still weighed a lot.

"Dizzy..."

"That happens sometimes." The twins looked up at Julius who was rummaging in his pocket. He pulled out a coloured candy that looked a bit like a candy cane but was shaped like a star and handed it to Daniel who had a hungry expression. Kyla could have sworn she saw a little bit of drool escape from his lips.

Her brother chewed on the candy as a test. "Wow." He breathed, devouring the whole thing in a matter of seconds, and straightening to look around.

"Better?" Julius grinned.

"I'm not dizzy anymore!" Daniel said, full of surprise.

"What did you give him?" Kyla asked.

"Swirldles. It helps stop the dizziness after going through light. It happens the first few times you travel by portals."

"How come I wasn't affected?" Kyla queried, thinking of the all too soothing sensation of the teleportation.

"Not everyone is affected, and it's never been proven why people don't get dizzy," Julius explained. "But there are speculations."

He stared at her for only a few seconds, but it felt like an eternity and when he didn't elaborate on the "speculations", Kyla had to resist the urge to ask. She brought her arms closer, shivering slightly from the cold; or maybe it was from the flood of questions forming in her mind.

"Where are we?" Daniel asked and Kyla knew he had noticed Julius' lack of information too, though he was obviously not going to ask him about it. Instead of asking questions Daniel was always the one to change subjects, not wanting to pressure anyone.

"My home." Julius nodded to the left. "Well not yet. We have a little walk to go on first."

It wasn't that long of a walk to his house, but Kyla's legs were too exhausted to agree, and started wobbling when they were only a couple of metres away. His home was huge compared to the twin's old home. It had at least 4 floors, from what she could tell: maybe even more! The glittering white walls were polished to perfection and glinted in the silver light projected by the rising moon, shining slightly. A cosmic garden surrounded the house, enlightening the view with its beautiful evergreens and flowers, which seemed to glow in the darkness. Water poured from the majestic fountain, situated in the middle of the pathway, creating a peaceful atmosphere once more and easing Kyla's worries ever so slightly.

"Wow!" Daniel was in awe of the place, gasping at the size of the house. "You live here?"

"No." Julius said sarcastically.

He smiled and winked, motioning for the twins to follow him forward. Julius led the way down the marble pathway, smiling as Kyla stared around the place, wide eyed. He put his hand in his pant pockets and fished out a small disk. It was silver with an emerald, green gem in the middle, surrounded by intricate red swirls. Julius placed it on the handle and 4 thin metal pieces shot out from below. A keyboard sprang from the middle of the door and Julius typed some kind of password, though Kyla didn't know which, as she had already turned around to give him some privacy. She wasn't the type of person who stared at people while they wrote their passwords, desperate to remember them and use them whenever she wished. Daniel on the other hand was leaning forward trying to see what was getting typed but Kyla grabbed him by the arm and dragged him back.

The door opened with a CLICK. Kyla and Daniel turned towards Julius as he said, "In you go." and closed the door behind them.

# CHAPTER 4 - KYLA



"Where have you been?" A voice asked from the shadows as Kyla, Daniel and Julius stepped through the door, away from the chilly breezes and into the nice warm air of the house. They jumped. The lights suddenly turned on, blinding Kyla for a second as her eyes struggled to adjust. From the corner of her eye, she could see the blurry silhouettes of Julius and her brother struggling as well, placing their hands over their eyes.

"So? Where have you been?" A teenage girl, around the same age as Kyla, stepped down from the steps in the corner. She had dark red hair with dark purple streaks and beautiful emerald, green eyes like Julius. The resemblance was impossible to miss and yet she seemed even more sure of herself. She stood tall and confident, striding towards them with steady steps, her eyes intimidating Kyla and making her take a step back.

"Nice to see you too." Julius mumbled, earning an exaggerated eye roll from the girl. "What are you doing up?"

"Nice try dodging my question. Where have you BEEN?" She spoke sharply and looked extremely serious, which was hard considering that she was wearing pyjamas with pink unicorns and fluffy bunnies. When Kyla looked down at the girl's feet, she also noticed that she was wearing adorable butterfly slippers, which made her look even less intimidating than before.

"Kyla, Daniel, this is Mackenzie, my daughter. Mackenzie, this is Kyla and Daniel. I suspect that they are very tired and would like to go to bed to rest," Kyla opened her mouth to argue that sleep was the last thing her brother and she wanted to do but Julius ignored her and continued talking to his daughter. "Can we please discuss this in the morning? I will fill you in on everything." Julius said, patiently and with a soft voice as if this was kind of like a daily routine for him.

"Everything. You'll tell me absolutely everything. You promise?" Mackenzie insisted, eyeing her dad, until he finally gave a small nod. Then she turned to the twins and gave them a bright smile. "Come on then. I'll take you to your room."

Kyla turned towards Julius, who dipped his chin in a slight nod and said with a smile "Good night, guys. See you up and ready early tomorrow morning!"

"Good night." She replied and Daniel copied her shyly. Kyla knew there was no point in trying to argue with Julius. She looked up at him trying to thank him for his hospitality and he smiled. Then she followed Mackenzie up the stairs, who climbed them two steps at a time, with real ease. It was a glittery, spiralling staircase, winding up several feet, with a decorative flowery carpet on every step. The walls also had soft flowery designs, though they were very faint and without much colour, making the house look even more elegant than it looked from the outside.

Kyla hurried up the steps to catch up with Mackenzie, Daniel right behind her. She kept trying to climb two steps at a time like Mackenzie but after tripping over several times, she had to give up and go up one at a time instead. She kept thinking about how her mom must be.

Trapped.

Hopeless.

Vulnerable.

Each word stabbed her harder and had her clutching her stomach. But the thing that hurt the most was knowing how stubborn she acted and how that might have been the last thing she had ever done towards her mom. She remembered what Icarus had told her. She had to stay calm. Positive. Happy.

For Daniel. For their mom.

"You, ok?" Kyla looked up, burying the dark thoughts in a far-off place in her mind. She would not think about her mom. She wouldn't like that.

Mackenzie was frowning down at her from the top of the stairs, staring at where her hand had been rubbing her messy knot of emotions. Her brother also looked at her, his brows furrowed together with worry.

"Yeah." She lied. She lowered her eyes as Mackenzie narrowed her stare. If she had any suspicions, she didn't say them out loud, as she motioned for the twins to follow her into the small corridor ahead. The walls had intricate drawings and pictures hung on huge golden frames. Kyla stopped and stared at a portrait of a young girl, with a perfect braid and dazzling green eyes.

"Is that you?" She asked Mackenzie who turned to look at where she was pointing.

"Yep. That was two years ago. Can we skip the house tour for tomorrow morning?" She didn't wait for an answer but kept walking down the corridor at a quick pace, the ears of her bunny slippers bobbing up and down with the movement. Kyla stole another quick glance at the portrait next to it; a young woman with auburn hair and light brown eyes holding a baby and smiling. Kyla had a good idea of who she could be and a look at Daniel told her he thought so too.

Kyla heard Mackenzie muttering "Where did they go

now?" and so rushed the way she went, turning a soft corner and walking straight to her. Literally. She walked straight into her.

"Ow." They cried in unison, both shaking their heads, where they had banged into each other. Daniel snickered behind them, earning himself a glare from Mackenzie.

Mackenzie got to her feet first, grabbing Kyla by the hands, and pulling her forward towards a door. She unlocked it and lightly pushed Kyla and Daniel inside, quietly closing the door behind them. She walked away and opened what looked like a huge closet, stepping inside, and leaving the twins to observe the room. It was quite spacious with a big queen-sized bed and a nice blue carpet laid in the middle of the room. A yellow sofa stood off to one side and the walls were nicely decorated with paintings and sketches of flowers and animals. Her favourite was one of a cheetah looking out at the sunset with her baby cubs.

Kyla was so focused on the painting that she didn't notice Mackenzie was next to her until she threw something at her head. The fabric slid down her stunned face and landed at her feet in a pile. She bent down and picked the clothes up, which she could now see were fresh pyjamas. They were almost identical to Mackenzie's but instead of unicorns and bunnies they were bright blue with mermaids and underwater creatures. They were also long sleeved, which was great as Kyla was freezing in the unusual weather of this new world. Mackenzie threw some clothes at Daniel, who seemed a bit distracted and only barely managed to catch them.

"There is another room for you." Mackenzie told him.

"Great." He replied and they both turned to Kyla, who stood, still not knowing what to do with the room.

"What are you waiting for? Get dressed." With that Mackenzie left the room, dragging Daniel out with her who said good night and that he would see her in the morning. Once Mackenzie had shut the door Kyla started getting dressed, putting on the buttons and folding up the ends of her pants which were slightly too big for her. She went into the bathroom that looked like those in a very fancy hotel, and washed her face, drying it off with a light pink towel.

Kyla was done, yet she didn't walk over to the bed and sleep. How could she when her mom was in danger? She lingered in the corner of the room then sighed.

Her mom wouldn't want her worrying. She wouldn't want her wasting her hours of sleep thinking about her.

Kyla took a deep breath and trudged over to bed, wrapping the warm covers around her and immediately falling asleep;

all her worries and concerns buried under a 'worry about later' part of her brain. Right now, the only thing she needed was a dreamless sleep.

And luckily, it came easily.

***

"Get up sleepy head." A voice spoke from far away.

But not far enough to ignore.

Kyla tossed and turned, pulling her pillow over her ears, trying to block out the voice as she tried to get a few extra minutes of sleep, but the voice kept right on bothering her.

"I said I'd see you early in the morning."

She groaned and slowly opened her tired eyes to a blaring amount of sunlight. For a minute all she saw was an intense glare of white light but then she rubbed her eyes and the whiteness cleared. Her eyes adjusted, finally settling onto a pair of familiar brown eyes.

"One more minute." Kyla moaned, not caring about the embarrassment later to come. She closed her eyes and fell onto the softness of her bed once more.

"Ok, you asked for it." Another voice warned but Kyla didn't care.

"Mhmmm." She mumbled, a yawn escaping through her lips, as she settled close to sleep once more. The peaceful, beautiful darkness came closer. Closer. Closer...

"AAAAAAH!" A very cold liquid dripped down her body, chilling her bones and jolting her awake almost immediately. Mackenzie, already dressed in a white dress, was standing in front of her bed, an evil grin on her face and trying very hard not to laugh. Her shoulders were shaking with laughter as Kyla mustered the best glare she could and yanked the soaking covers from around her. Daniel was also there trying not to laugh but a couple of snorts escaped, and he was soon laughing hysterically at Kyla's dripping wet pyjamas.

"Get dressed, we're going to see my dad's friend." Mackenzie frowned as if disgusted by the idea for some reason. "Oh, and sorry for waking you."

"Don't worry about it. I'll get my revenge." Kyla smirked, looking at both culprits, then got up to change, grabbing the clothes that were left on her bedside table and walking over to the bathroom. The choice of clothes was a bit different from what she would have chosen but she put them on anyhow. First, she pulled the red dress over her head, then she slipped on the denim jacket as she was sure it was still freezing cold outside the house. She slid her feet into a pair of black boots and started brushing her hair into a half up-half down, braided hairstyle, which made her red strands stand out.

Kyla quickly made her way downstairs, arriving in the living room with Julius and Mackenzie already dressed and waiting for her. Julius had even gelled his hair to perfection, which looked amazingly natural.

He nodded when he saw her. "You look great."

"Uh... thanks" She stammered, a light shade of red rising up her cheeks at the compliment.

"How did you sleep?"

Shame swelled inside her as she muttered a quick "ok". Instead of frowning Julius smiled with relief.

"Good." Then he added "No need to feel ashamed, your mother wouldn't want that." It was as if he could read her thoughts.

Mackenzie went over to Kyla and muttered "Everything is going to be ok." But Kyla wasn't so sure, so she didn't say anything, and a sense of uncomfortable silence settled over them until Daniel made his way down the stairs, grinning as he saw Kyla's jaw drop.

"What did you do to your hair?" She asked.

"Do you like it?" He wriggled his eyebrows, which made

his gelled-up hair demand more attention. It really brought out the green spikes in between the brown.

Kyla was about to reply when Julius interrupted them, reminding everyone that they should probably leave if they wanted to arrive on time. Kyla noticed that Mackenzie sighed again, looking very displeased with the idea of going wherever they were going.

They walked out and around the community of houses following Julius and Daniel who walked faster than any of them. Kyla, meanwhile, chose to fall into step with Mackenzie, finally bringing up the question that had been bugging her for so long.

"So what's up?"

"Nothing." Mackenzie said with a snap, then forced a smile.

"Really?" Kyla raised an eyebrow with a grin. "Every time someone mentions where we're going you cringe. Do you not like your dad's friend?"

Mackenzie grimaced and for a second it seemed that the conversation was dead and that she was going to ignore the question completely. Kyla was about to change the subject to make things less uncomfortable when Mackenzie spoke.

"It's not that I don't like his friend, it's that his son is very annoying..."

"Annoying how?"

She opened her mouth then shut it as if she couldn't be bothered to explain. "Well, you'll see."

Mackenzie seemed like the most open and loving person and the fact that she didn't like the son, worried Kyla. What if he was mean? What if he was one of those horrible bullies that made everyone's lives difficult?

On the other hand, he might be really nice and hopefully become Daniel's friend. That would be great for him. It would make him forget all about the last 24 hours...

She was so caught up in her own thoughts that she didn't see where she was going and almost slammed into a door, earning a snicker from her brother. She looked up and found a house, very much like Julius' but with beautiful flowers and decorative plants all around the front door. Many purple orchids hung near the edge of the door, and Julius lifted them up slowly, revealing a silver disk underneath. He pushed it and a soft DING echoed off the device.

Almost instantly, the door was flung open, and a young woman stepped out. She had the most dazzling cobalt blue eyes and bright blonde hair with azure streaks that was styled into a neat bun. It looked like she was ready for work with a smart blue blazer and a short white skirt. She reminded Kyla so much of her mom that it was almost painful.

The woman smiled upon seeing them at her doorstep. "Good morning!" she said, greeting them, first Julius then Mackenzie and finally she stopped in front of the twins.

"Who might you be?" She asked them.

"I'm Daniel."

"Kyla."

The woman's eyes widened to their fullest and she turned toward Julius who gave a slight nod. A silent understanding seemed to pass between them, and Kyla struggled to guess what was going on. She saw Daniel's eyes narrow ever so slightly but when he caught her looking, he shrugged.

Before Kyla could open her mouth to ask, the woman smiled, showing her perfect white teeth.

"My name is Gwenda." She spoke. "Now what are we waiting for? Come on in."

***

"MOM! KALEN WON'T GIVE ME THE REMOTE!" A screech echoed off the walls making everyone apart from Gwenda flinch. She just sighed and motioned the others to follow her down the wide corridor.

"It's my turn to choose." Another voice called, much softer than the last. "You know that."

More shouts were thrown around. The two boys kept arguing; one of them even started to cry what sounded very much like huge depressing sobs for their mom to hear.

"I'm gone for five minutes, and this is what happens." Gwenda groaned once they'd reached the room furthest from the front door. Kyla could hear the shouts more clearly now, louder, and more extreme.

"William, I told you already. No."

Gwenda rubbed her temples and took a deep breath to steady herself. Then she tentatively opened the door to reveal two boys.

The first was around Kyla and Daniel's age. He had blond hair with ice blue streaks, curled at the front and sparkling ice-blue eyes the same colour as his hair, which seemed to be the case for lots of shapeshifters. Due to his anger, his eyebrows were knitted at the front, but he still managed to look calm and in control. The other boy was slightly younger, maybe around 12 years old and identical to his brother; with the same blonde hair but with a darker shade of blue mixed in and ice blue eyes. The only real difference was their heights.

As the boys heard the door shut behind them, they turned and noticed the audience standing there, watching. Gwenda glared at her two sons, whilst rapidly tapping her foot in frustration.

The younger boy dropped down on his knees rather dramatically. "He won't give me the remote."

"He chose the show yesterday." The other boy sighed. They both bickered back and forth for at least a minute, until their mother finally stepped in.

"Stop it! Both of you!" She scolded. "Give me that!" She marched forwards and yanked the remote out of the boy's hands, flinging it across the room and onto a table on the back corner, where it landed perfectly upright.

"Seriously, behave yourselves! You're acting like little kids!" She shrieked, then glanced at her guests and gave a small, embarrassed smile. "We have guests."

Both boys' faces turned a flaming shade of red as they noticed Kyla and Daniel, standing behind Gwenda, and trying very hard to not be seen. It didn't work though. Kyla felt herself blush, taking a strand of her hair and playing around with it to distract herself. She did not like tense atmospheres.

"Boys, this is Kyla and Daniel." Gwenda said, spreading her arms in a dramatic way. "Guys this is William and Kalen".

She pointed at the youngest son first, then landed her finger on the oldest; "Kalen" as if gathering her thoughts. A light bulb seemed to switch on in her mind and her smile broadened.

"Kalen is actually the same age as you, so why don't you follow him up to his room and get to know each other?"

Kyla wondered exactly how Gwenda knew her age, but decided not to ask and so turned, following Kalen out of the room. Standing next to him, she could see that they were around the same height, him being a little bit taller because of the tips of hair standing up. Daniel was obviously shorter by a full head. The children spent a few seconds in uncomfortable silence, until Kyla had the courage to clear her throat.

"That was quite an argument with your brother." She spoke. Kalen's whole face turned bright red, and he looked down at his feet.

"Yeah, sorry about that."

Daniel laughed good- heartedly.

"Don't be. I know siblings can be tough sometimes" he said pointing at Kyla, who stuck her tongue out at him.

"Siblings are rough." Kyla and Daniel jumped, almost tripping over themselves. Mackenzie was right behind them grinning mischievously. "I feel bad for poor William, having a brother like you."

"Ha. Ha." Kalen said sarcastically. " I feel bad for your dad. All alone with no one else but you."

Mackenzie glared at him and rolled her eyes, obviously bitter that he had come up with a response- even if it was a kind of lame one. Kyla had to resist putting her hand over her mouth and laughing. Her shoulders shook nonetheless and she decided to change the subject.

"Where's your room?" She asked Kalen.

"Right here." He paused in front of an oakwood door. He placed his hand over the doorknob and carefully turned it, pushing it inwards and motioning for his guests to walk in.

Makenzie raced forward but the twins stayed at the door. Kyla could see her friend inspecting every corner of the room, frowning ever so slightly until she spotted something to the right. She laughed.

"Seriously?" Makenzie could hardly contain her laughter as her eyes glistened with tears.

Kalen walked into the room and Kyla decided to follow him, rather tentatively, Daniel following in her footsteps. She had no idea what Makenzie was laughing at and was a bit afraid to find out. She turned her body so she was facing the same way the others were but couldn't find anything disturbing. There was only a huge poster of some sports team with an eagle logo, hung up on the emerald, green walls.

"I have no idea what you're laughing about." Kalen said to Makenzie with a serious expression, his brows scrunched together.

She laughed. "You support 'The Eagles'?'" She laughed harder. "Pathetic. They're so pathetic."

Kalen's cheeks burned with fury. "They are not pathetic. In fact, they are at the top of the league. What team do you support again? Oh yeah. The falcons! What place are they?"

He paused, tapping his finger over his mouth as if trying to recall. "That's right! They are currently tenth!" He laughed bitterly.

Makenzie frowned and opened her mouth to reply but Daniel stepped in asking the question Kyla was about to ask, "What are you guys talking about?"

They both stopped and turned towards him simultaneously, with mouths wide open. Talk about…Creepy.

Kalen recovered from the shock first, shaking his head. "How do you not know what they are?"

"Of course, he doesn't know. They both don't know." Makenzie said, rolling her eyes dramatically. "They lived on

Earth."

"Earth?" he asked. "The small planet in the middle of nowhere?"

Makenzie nodded sympathetically. Then she brightened into her old self. "What we're talking about are teams in the Changeball league."

She leant towards the twins and whispered, "The falcons are the better team."

Kyla didn't really hear what she said as she was busy trying to figure out how to ask what Changeball was. Turned out she didn't have to as Kalen realised her expression a split second after.

"Changeball is a sport we like." He grinned as Kyla fumbled for a reassurance that she knew what that was. Daniel on the other hand didn't seem embarrassed.

"How do you play?" he asked intrigued. He loved sports and Kyla knew that he would beg to play as soon as possible.

As Kalen explained the overly complicated rules, Kyla's eyes wandered over the wall of splattered posters. Over the green walls, bed, and couch. Over the photos lying about, until she noticed one of Kalen with a young man, around the same age as his mom. He had brushed back blonde hair with dark blue strands, styled mostly to the left, his mouth forming a huge smile as he posed for the camera.

"Is that your dad?" Kyla asked, interrupting Kalen's latest explanation of the Changeball sport.

"Yep." He spoke. "He works at school, same as my mom. He takes care of some of the magical creatures for our magical creatures' teacher."

"What does your mom work as?" Daniel spoke, staring at the picture Kyla had been studying a few seconds before.

"She's the principal for the school."

Suddenly, Gwenda's knowledge of the twin's age made sense and Kyla felt herself smiling, relieved to know the principal of their new school was so kind.

"Yeah, a really strict one." Mackenzie mumbled with disgust.

"Only because you have a bad reputation." Kalen said defensively. "In our old school she would get detention like every week."

"You did?" Kyla and Daniel asked, though Kyla sounded more distasteful whilst Daniel sounded deeply impressed.

"What did you do?" He asked eagerly.

"Join me and I'll tell you." She replied with a mischievous grin.

"I can join?"

"NO!" Kyla snapped at the same time Mackenzie replied "Of course!"

Kyla glared at her, but she only grinned even more, her eyes sparkling with a nervous energy that was now reflected in Daniel.

Kyla groaned.

"I knew it was only a matter of time before she started her own trouble making gang." Kalen said with a sigh.

"I'm scared to think of what havoc they might cause together." Kyla agreed.

"Someone should warn the school."

"As soon as possible."

Kyla and Kalen shared a smile and from then on, Kyla knew that they would become good friends. The four of them.

A knock sounded from the door, and it opened a second later to allow Gwenda through.

"Anyone want lemonade?" She held up a tray with five glasses of the sour yellow liquid and each of the teens grabbed one, leaving the spare on the tray.

She cleared her throat. "Daniel, Kyla. Julius told me about what happened, and I want you both to know that if you need anything" She emphasised the word looking at both twins in turn. "Come to me. Our home is your home."

Kyla's eyes burned with tears, but she fought against them, willing herself to stay strong in front of Mackenzie and Kalen.

"Anyway, since you are both starting school tomorrow..."

"TOMORROW?"

"Yes, tomorrow." Gwenda continued. "I figured you would need supplies and since I'm the principal I have a few extras you can use down in the basement. Kalen, would you help them?"

"Of course." He grinned.

"And Mackenzie since I'm sure you have already managed to lose some of the things you need, I suggest you also have a look around."

"Yes madam." Mackenzie mocked and Gwenda playfully pushed her, rumpling up her hair so much it covered her face. When she surfaced her face was as red as her hair.

"No mischief." Gwenda ordered staring at both Mackenzie and Daniel and making Kyla wonder how she knew her brother was a troublemaker even before she met him. She must have a sixth sense or something.

"Yeah right." Mackenzie and Daniel mumbled under their breaths at the same time. They looked up at each other and winked.

Kalen smiled at his mom, who was staring at Daniel and Mackenzie, and motioned for everyone to follow him out the door. He led them down the corridor, past his brother who looked up, then looked away hurriedly as Kyla's eyes met his, and towards a spacious room. He stopped short of the room, kneeling, and taking out a small square gadget which he placed in a small rectangle on the wooden floor. Blue light flowed around the square and a panel slid open revealing a set of stairs leading down.

"Careful where you step." Kalen warned them, placing a step onto the first block, and making his way down. Mackenzie followed, jumping down the steps and not being careful at all. Daniel looked at Kyla and she signalled for him to go next, which he did, carefully stepping one step after another in the darkness.

It was Kyla's turn and she followed him. Or tried to but she couldn't see a thing at first and so tripped over her boots and got thrown forward. Her vision improved rapidly, and she saw herself getting closer to hitting the floor. Luckily a pair of hands grabbed her by the arm and put her upright just in time, preventing a face plant on the hard wooden floor.

"Thanks." She whispered, pulling away from Kalen.

"No problem." He assured her. "I forgot that you guys

don't have night vision yet."

"Night vision?" Daniel asked.

"Yeah. All shapeshifters can see in the dark as well as having a better scent, hearing, and other things. But it takes a lot of practice, which you guys obviously haven't had. The more you shapeshift the more animal characteristics you get."

A clap echoed around them, and an iridescent light blared on, illuminating the basement, which was full of big cardboard boxes. Mackenzie stood to the left; her hands clasped together.

"Can we please get started?" She asked, redoing the bow on her white dress.

"Ok so just look around." Kalen told the twins. "Oh wait, I think I have the school supply list somewhere around here... AHA!"

He handed Kyla a slip of clear white paper and she read it aloud for Daniel to hear.

*Supplies:*

*Formal or fancy clothes for special school year occasions as well as uniforms.*

*One weapon of your choice. (Must be forged at school)*

*The Woodford encyclopaedia of Creatures.*

*Book on Shapeshifting: the theory and Shapeshifting: A history.*

*Dome Hologram set 2821.*

*The rest will be handed to you by your teachers, given below.*

*Subjects:*

*Study of Mythical Creatures and Demons. Professor - Ms Piper Orgi*

*Self Defence. Professor - Mr Sedgwick Smithy.*

*Strategy. Professor - Ms Cecelia Pomieko.*

*History. Professor - Mr Osbourne Butland*

*Life skills. Professor - Ms Nicola Hinkle.*

*Practical Shapeshifting. Professor - Monsieur Pris*

*Armoury. Professor - Mr Teeny Alpesh*

*Yours most sincerely Principal Smith. See you soon.*

"Wow." Kyla breathed. "What are life skills?"

"Seriously? That's what you're most shocked by?" Daniel asked. "What about the fact that a teacher is called Mr Butland? I mean what kind of name is that?"

"I know right?" Mackenzie cracked up.

Kalen rolled his eyes at both of them, turning to answer Kyla's question. "Life skills include many things like potions, simple spells, disguises and so on. I guess they didn't come up with a really good name so settled on calling it Life Skills."

"Yeah, I doubt Potions/Simple spells/Disguises/ etc is a catchy name." Daniel said. He snickered at his own humour as did Mackenzie beside him and Kyla ignored them both, turning towards the only other mature one in the room.

"Your last name is Smith?" Kyla asked Kalen.

"Yeah. My name is Kalen Cato Smith."

"Cato?"

"Don't laugh! I'll have you know it means all knowing."

"Yeah, because you're definitely some kind of genius." Mackenzie said sarcastically with a roll of her eyes.

Kalen opened his mouth to snap back at her, but Kyla interrupted them.

"Where can we find the supplies?"

"Just look around, though I don't think you'll find any fancy clothes. I can probably lend Daniel some but not you."

"I can give you some when we get back home. Same as some casual clothes. Or I can just ask my dad if we can go to a shop to buy them." Mackenzie offered and Kyla mustered a smile, but the word 'home' still affected her. She didn't feel at home without her mom.

Uncomfortable silence followed, as everyone's minds darkened with that realisation, broken only when Kalen told them to look around. Kyla forced herself to move about, opening some boxes and looking inside for the supplies listed on the paper. Daniel trailed behind her.

In the next few minutes both Daniel and Kyla had everything on the list apart from three things: their fancy clothes, school uniform and their weapons, seeing as they had to be crafted at school.

"I'll ask my dad if we can take you shopping later today." Mackenzie told them once they had explained what they had gathered. "Maybe we could go get your fancy clothes too while we're at it."

"Maybe I can come too!" Kalen added excitedly.

Mackenzie frowned. "Do you have to?"

Everyone laughed and the mood suddenly shifted to a happier, lighter one, where Kyla didn't feel stressed or fidgety. They made their way back upstairs and to the living room, where they found William sitting on the couch in the corner reading a book and the adults in a conversation, which stopped as they spotted the unexpected audience.

"Are you guys all set?" Julius asked with a smile.

"Actually, we were wondering if you could take us to the city. Kyla and Daniel need their uniforms." Mackenzie said.

"How about we go this afternoon after lunch?"

"Can I come too?" Kalen asked his mom and his brother's head snapped up as she nodded.

"Can I go?" He asked, closing his book.

"Why don't you ask them?" Gwenda said.

"Can I come?" William mumbled, staring at his feet shyly.

"Of course!" Kyla and Daniel beamed. Mackenzie on the other hand was shaking her head saying that one 'Smith' boy was enough to handle but everyone ignored her, and William jumped to his feet happily.

"Unfortunately, I have work to do in preparation for school..." Gwenda started but Julius cut her off.

"It would be my pleasure to take care of them."

"Thank you but please let me make it up to you with a discount for Restaurantastic."

"SERIOUSLY?" Mackenzie, Kalen, and William shrieked.

"It's the least I can do."

"What's Restaurantastic?" Kyla couldn't help asking. The name felt really really cringy.

"Only the best restaurant in Ocelia!" Mackenzie said. "You'll love it!"

Daniel's mouth hung open and Kyla swore she heard a rumbling sound coming from where he stood.

"Well, it's twelve o'clock now so what do you say we get some lunch?" Julius laughed as they all shouted "Yes!" and before they knew it, they were out the door, waving goodbye to Gwenda as they walked past the pastures and followed Julius down the pathway.

# CHAPTER 5

# **DANIEL**

"Are we there yet?" Daniel moaned, clutching his hungry stomach which seemed to growl more with the overly repeated question. They had been walking for what felt like eternity.

The Restaurantastic had better be worth it because so far its name does not hold much promise. Daniel thought bitterly.

"No." Julius replied for what had to be the tenth time in the last five minutes.

"Again." Mackenzie said, gritting her teeth so much it looked hurtful. "You'll know because you'll see a sign. And do you know what the sign will say?"

Daniel rolled his eyes, choosing to ignore her which turned out to be the wrong decision as it only angered her more.

"RESTAURANTASTIC! IT WOULD SAY RESTAURANTASTIC!"

"Can you both just stop already?" Kyla cried, pulling her hair over her ears as if that would save her from hearing their bickering.

"Seriously." Kalen agreed, walking beside Kyla with William nearby. "We're all hungry you know?"

"You have to be patient." Julius spoke from where he was leading them forward.

"Can't we go by car?" Daniel suggested.

"We don't have cars here. We mostly use Caravans with customizable insides."

"Cool." The twins breathed.

"And besides, we're almost there."

"You've been saying that for the past twenty minutes." William pointed out. He seemed to be finding the long walk harder than any of them, although to be fair he did have the shortest legs. Sweat beaded his forehead and he kept waving his hand in front of his face, hoping to create a bit of a wind.

"Well, there it is." Julius pointed to a large purple building in front of them. At first glance it looked like a purple blob with a bad hair day but when you looked closely it could be said that it resembled an octopus. Its large tentacles towered overhead, and the door opened and closed as if they were teeth.

"Whoa" breathed Daniel, his eyes scanning the giant building beaming down at him.

"Good afternoon, and welcome to Restaurantastic. How may I help you?" The attendant smiled but it looked painfully forced as if her cheeks would explode from the strain.

Julius smiled, showing all his teeth. "We would like a table for six please."

"Coming right up." She went over, opened a secret compartment in the octopus' tentacle and grabbed a handful of what looked like menus made of seaweed. She opened the front door, Julius right behind her and the children followed, eager for food.

Inside was amazing! Daniel loved everything! He loved the water designed floor! He loved the black ink-shaped tables, and he especially loved the tentacle shaped seats arranged for their group in one of the middle tables!

"Wow." Kyla breathed, her eyes glittering with admiration.

"Sit down kids."

Daniel reached towards the same chair as Mackenzie, their hands touching as they both placed them on the chair. Daniel really felt like taking the chair for himself but instead he acted 'the gentleman' and pulled it back for her, sitting on the opposite side next to Kyla and Julius.

"The menus." Julius passed the menus around the table first to Daniel, Kyla, Kalen, William and finally to his daughter, who flipped through it hungrily.

"What are you thinking of ordering?" Kyla asked William, who blushed as he closed the kid's menu.

"Fish and chips. Kids meal."

"Ooh. That sounds good but I think I'll order some sushi." She said. Then she added, "With fries of course."

"I'm going for salmon." Kalen said.

"Seabass with seaweed for me I think." Daniel told Julius and Kyla gagged rudely.

"Seriously? Worst combination ever!" She told him.

"It's actually really good." Daniel snapped back.

"Hmhm. Whatever you say." She turned back to her menu, completely ignoring him.

"I think I'll go with fish fingers with fries and crab sticks." Mackenzie said and when her eyes met Daniel's she smiled. He knew she was thanking him for letting her sit where she sat and so smiled back.

"Ok. I'll call the waitress."

The same waitress came over, her blonde with plum

strands hair pulled back in a bun that told Daniel she meant business. She took their order, frowning at Daniel's choice and having him mentally shout IT'S NOT A WEIRD COMBINATION! He glared at her until she left towards what he assumed was the kitchen.

"So, are you excited for school?" Julius asked the twins. Daniel eyed Kyla who tried to look confident but ended up mumbling.

"It's going to be weird being new."

Mackenzie and Kalen howled with laughter. Even William and Julius cracked a smile.

"What?" Daniel and Kyla asked frustrated. "What's so funny?" They stared at each other. Talk about a twin moment.

"That's what you're scared of?" Kalen asked, drying the tears that had sprang from the laughter. Daniel and Kyla looked at each other and Daniel forced himself to nod, Kyla doing the same thing.

"Well, then you have nothing to worry about." Julius assured them.

"What do you mean?" Daniel asked and just then sounds of plates getting dragged sounded nearby and Daniel lifted his eyes, gasping at what he saw.

Miniscule slides had appeared above them, and different

sized splotches of paint moved along- no, not splotches of paint. Plates. Their meals were coming towards them, sliding down the twisting metal and landing on each of the coloured mats assigned to each of them. A green ink shaped plate landed in front of Daniel with a delicious looking dish: a long white fish surrounded by sheets of dark green seaweed.

He could see that Kyla's pink plate contained twelve miniscule sushi pieces which she admired, turning the plate around to see every detail better. Mackenzie's blue plate contained rectangular strips of fried fish with fries off to one side, whilst Kalen's just had a fish with a very colourful flesh, ranging from orange to dark red and William's red plate was populated with slices of flowered fish with chips on the side.

Daniel cut into his food. "Mmmm." He whispered, starting to gobble up the rest of his meal. The fish tasted salty but also had a tint of soy sauce which made it have a unique taste. Kyla mimed vomiting as he dropped the dark brown liquid onto the fish, but Daniel didn't care.

"What do you mean we have nothing to worry about?" Kyla asked, taking one of the sushi using tentacle chopsticks and placing it in her mouth, closing her eyes as she ate.

"If that's what you're worried about then you're stressing over nothing." Mackenzie said through a mouthful of crab sticks.

"What do you mean?"

"It's the first year for everyone." Kalen explained, taking a sip of water. "Before that we went to a prep school but now, we're all starting at a higher level as almost everyone would be used to their talents by now."

"Oh." Kyla and Daniel sighed in relief, which quickly vanished as Daniel realised something.

"But we're not used to our powers."

"Don't worry." Julius said. "I have a feeling you two are quick learners."

He smiled as he said it, but Daniel didn't find the words reassuring and he could tell Kyla didn't either as she dropped her eyes to her lap and spun her food around with her chopsticks. William looked up at her, then continued eating his fish and chips.

"So, William." Julius said, changing the subject. "You will start at this school next year too. Are you excited?"

"I guess." The sound of cutlery on plates was the only noise over the next minute.

"What school do you go to now?" Kyla asked, leaning over to grab some soy sauce for her sushi.

"A prep school."

"Do you like it?"

"Yeah." He replied, whilst wiping his mouth on a seaweed napkin.

"What's school like?" Daniel asked Julius, hopefully sparing William from any more questions. William glanced up at him with a relieved smile. Mackenzie meanwhile, began to explain the school.

"They have this great sports staff for Changeball. The coach is said to have trained some of the best world players and this year we can try out for the team, though I don't think they'll choose us, since we're so young and new and most likely have played a lot less than the others but..."

"Mackenzie. I think Daniel meant the classes." Julius told her and she looked at a loss of words, looking down at her already-finished meal.

Daniel had asked about the classes but now he felt fully intrigued and wanted to know more about Changeball instead.

"I think I'll order the bill and then, what do you say we go shopping?" Julius pressed a button in the middle of the table and a few seconds later the waitress arrived with a slip of paper, waiting for payment.

Daniel couldn't quite hide his groan at the thought of

wandering around, trying on clothes, looking at girly dresses…

"I might buy you a little treat." Julius whispered and Daniel perked up, leaving the restaurant before anyone else and entering the purple portal emitted from the bubble in Julius' hand which was their ride to the city.

***

"Let's go get you a uniform."

"Can we go buy Changeball stuff?"

"We need to get your books."

Families crowded the streets of the city where the twins found themselves in. Children clung to their parent's sleeves, pointing towards the windows of certain shops, and begging them to take a look at the latest video game or change ball gloves (which Daniel loved). Kalen appeared through the teleportation circle next, patting his hair and rumpling it, whilst Mackenzie strode out right behind him. She nudged Daniel's shoulder and pointed towards the centre of the square where a statue of a lady with a jewelled dress and a matching crown stood posing.

"Who's that?" Daniel jumped slightly, surprised at his sister's sudden appearance behind him. William stood next to her, his hair wild from the wind.

"Our ruler." Mackenzie rolled her eyes. Daniel should have gotten used to it by now as she did it every time she spoke. "Madame Lemoine."

"Madame Lemon?" Daniel asked, immediately picturing the extremely sour, bright citrus fruit with black and different coloured strands of hair curling around its 'face'. He shook his head, traumatised.

"Not Lemon." William laughed as Daniel's cheeks burned with embarrassment. "Le-moi-ne"

"Oh."

"If Ingrid heard you." Kalen said with a smile.

"Ingrid?" Kyla asked with a raised eyebrow.

"A girl in our year." He explained, then pointed to the statue as he said. "Her daughter."

Julius came up behind them and placed a hand on each of the twin's shoulders. "Ready to go?"

"Duh." Daniel replied as Kyla said "yes please" formally, shooting Daniel a shocked expression at his use of slang.

"Ok let's get you guys your uniforms at Black Wolf clothes." Julius whispered, taking Mackenzie's hand as they crossed the busy road.

Daniel decided to walk behind everyone, as they advanced

towards a large dark ware-house type shop. As soon as they set foot inside the store, an old woman carefully stepped forward, her wild hair flowing around her sharp features. Daniel couldn't help looking scared as the woman held out a bony hand and started measuring him with shaky hands. The woman smiled a toothless smile and snapped her fingers. Daniel looked in amazement- he was now wearing a tight black, sleek jumpsuit with a small leather pouch. He turned and saw that Kyla was wearing almost the exact design with the alteration of the crest next to her heart. Hers resembled a red, vicious dragon whilst Daniel's was a small multi-coloured lizard which he took as a chameleon. He also noticed that her shoulder patch was blank, as was his own when he looked at it.

"That is where your house team's sign will appear once you know which one you are in." The old woman squeaked with a soft voice as if reading Daniel's mind. "And in the winter, your sleeves will lengthen to keep you warm, so you won't need to wear a jumper in combat training."

"You guys look great!" Mackenzie said and Kalen, William and Julius nodded in agreement, making Kyla blush with the compliment. The old woman smiled at her and winked at Daniel.

Cheerily, Julius brushed forward and gave the old woman a few credits. The word Lion Hearts clung to the gold metal and Daniel realised that it must be the shapeshifter's currency. With a final toothless smile, the old woman was gone, and Daniel was being led outside by Kyla, who had her clothes back to normal and was clinging to him in the crowded streets.

Her eyes sparkled. "The uniforms are so cool."

"I know right?" William agreed bitterly. "Why can't my school have them?"

"Cheer up." Kalen told him, brushing his shoulder lightly. "You'll get one next year."

William beamed, giving his older brother a toothy grin before catching up with Julius at the front.

"Now for your fancy clothes." Julius shouted back over the blaring noise.

Daniel could've sworn he heard Kyla groan, and he couldn't blame her as his mind raced thinking of all the tight suits and ties and...

"It's not as bad as you think." Kalen whispered, making Daniel jump slightly.

"How would you know what I'm thinking?"

"Please." He laughed. "I've been there."

Somehow Daniel believed him.

"It's not as bad as you think." Kalen repeated.

Daniel didn't feel assured, but he didn't run away or try to escape from entering the lime-coloured store Julius brought them to. He stayed, choosing to give the shop a chance at making him buy 'fancy clothes'.

Mackenzie nudged the twins' forwards. "Well, look around."

They shrugged, probably thinking the same thing.

It can't hurt to have a look.

Kyla moved on to the women's section and Daniel ambled towards the coloured suits on the right.

Each looked shinier and fancier, with brighter colours like yellow and green, and frills on the sleeves. Daniel's eyes widened with each one and he felt himself flinch at the thought of wearing any of these over-the-top suits. One was even bright pink with multi-coloured sparkles.

SPARKLES!

He was about to give up hope of finding a better suit than the lime green one in his hand when his eyes rested on the best suit he'd ever seen- not that he'd seen many.

The suit in front of him was as sharp as a new knife and dyed to a gorgeous shade of deep navy- the same colour of a dark sky. There were no sparkles, no jewels. No colours that stood out. It was normal.

It was perfect.

He grabbed it, rushing over to the male's changing room and trying it on, staring at his reflection in the mirror and admiring how good it looked on him. He came out of the changing room needing a second opinion, to find Julius who grinned.

"I think you look awesome."

Daniel smiled. The sound of curtains opening sounded from the other end of the shop and Kyla stepped out in a flowing red dress, strapped around the neck and with a small tear from the ankle to the knee. It was the exact same scarlet red as her hair, and it suited her really well as she twirled in it. It seemed to sway with every step, and she posed dramatically in front of Julius, smiling as she asked how she looked.

"Perfect." He praised, making her face get camouflaged with the dress.

She turned to Daniel and looked at his outfit. "I think it suits you." She waited for him to say something. "Don't you get it? I said suits you because it's a suit and..."

"I get it." Daniel interrupted and Kyla stuck her tongue out at him, as he turned to get changed back into his plain green shirt and jeans. He came out of the changing area and handed Julius the suit, who told him to pick out a few ties to go with it.

Daniel asked Mackenzie to assist him as she had a pretty good style herself and they finally settled on a green, red, and dark blue tie. Mackenzie also dared him to choose a neon pink bow tie which came as an additional gift for their buys, and he couldn't resist it.

So out the shop they went, each of the twins carrying their large buys in a small black sphere, which the shop attendant explained still, somehow, contained their clothes, nicely ironed and in normal size. Daniel didn't really understand how but he chose not to ask, afraid his mind could not take the mind-blowing truth.

"Now for that treat I promised you." Julius said to Daniel once they had crossed the road.

"What treat?" Kyla asked.

"What would you like?"

Kyla shrugged, then an idea seemed to pop into her mind midway. "Do shapeshifters collect cards?"

"No." William said, who was once again standing next to her. "We do collect other things though."

"Can you show me?"

"Sure."

"Not so fast you two." Julius grabbed William by the arm before he could walk away. "You can't go alone. William you're too young and Kyla you don't know where you're going so how about Kalen goes with you guys. I think I remember him knowing a lot about collections."

William started to protest saying that he was only one year younger than Kalen, but Kyla shushed him as Kalen explained about all the collections he had made over the years and dragged both his brother and Kyla away, towards the stores.

"What would you like, Daniel?" Julius asked.

Before Daniel could reply Mackenzie frowned. "What should I get?"

"It's up to you." Julius reminded her.

Mackenzie thought for only a second, then her eyes sparkled. "Changeball trainers."

"You already have some." Julius argued.

"Please?" She begged. "They're broken and this year I can join the best team ever! Pretty Please?"

Julius hesitated but agreed after Mackenzie's continuous pleas and then he turned back to Daniel, awaiting an answer.

"I'm not sure." Daniel had a tempting idea in the back of his head, but it felt a bit foolish since he didn't even know how to play...

"You can think on the way." Mackenzie rushed forward, yelling at her father and Daniel to hurry up as she dodged the rushing parents and exhausted children, making her way towards a store at the end of the street.

A huge ball shaped building stood before Daniel. It was glassed with different colours ranging from bright orange to mustard yellow and it looked so cool! A sort of flame surrounded the crystal ball, changing colour as well, along with the height of the flames. Daniel looked up, reading the massive sign that said "CHANGEBALL WORLD".

"Come on." Mackenzie yanked Daniel forward by the arm, almost slamming him into the automatic door, which had yet to open. Even though it was only for a second, Mackenzie tapped her foot, frustrated. Then she raced inside, pulling Daniel with her without his consent.

Shelves of all shapes and sizes populated the gigantic room. No, not room. It was more the size of a great hall and not a single space on the wall was blank. If there were no more merchandise to sell, then tiny screens hung broadcasting the latest Changeball game. Daniel glanced at one of them, just as someone scored, letting the rapidly changing ball soar through the goal and into the back of the net.

Mackenzie let out a soft "Yes." And Daniel realised that it was her team playing- the falcons, playing against the rhinos. She turned rapidly and grabbed his arm as she pushed him further into a giant room filled with accessories and clothing. Immediately after, she started barraging him with questions.

"What do you want to play as? Have you chosen a favourite team yet? Do you want a shirt or something else? Hmm I think you're a medium size or are you a small?" she said as she started looking through the hanging pieces of sportswear.

"Um I used to play as goalie when I played football." He spoke. Mackenzie turned around and immediately grabbed a pair of pitch-black gloves, stuffing them into his hands.

"Perfect you can have these and when we get home, we can see just how good you are." Her eyes glinted evilly at this which made Daniel gulp in fear. He could see Julius giving him a warning look as if to say good luck kid but before he could ask what he meant, Mackenzie nudged him playfully.

"Try them on then."

Daniel sighed but slipped them through his fingers non the less, waiting for them to feel like normal football gloves but they didn't. They didn't feel like gloves. Daniel wriggled his fingers, clenching and relaxing his fists but it felt normal as if he didn't have any gloves on. His hands did feel surprisingly stronger somehow.

He was admiring the effect when Mackenzie shouted "Catch", throwing a crystal ball straight at a very expensive looking vase. Instinctively, Daniel dived towards it, arms outstretched, fingers extended and miraculously caught it, hugging it close to his chest as if to protect it from causing any harm.

He glared at Mackenzie who looked back at him quite innocently.

"What'd you do that for?" He asked her.

"Nice catch." She said, completely ignoring his question and walking over to the shoes section of the store. She picked out a pair of black trainers, with purple flames along the sides, yanked Daniels' gloves out of his hands and then handed them over to her dad, who went to the counter. A few seconds later he came back, giving Daniel a bag with his gloves but explaining that he had to wait for Mackenzie's trainers, which were getting cleaned.

Mackenzie walked over to the screens broadcasting the matches and groaned. "We're losing? Seriously?"

She looked really angry, like she was about to lash out and crack the screen in front of them. The shop attendant must've realised the same thing because a few seconds later he escorted them out, demanding that they wait outside for Julius.

"Did you get kicked out again?" A mocking voice asked behind them and Daniel turned to find Kalen, along with William and Kyla, who each held a bag in their hands.

"Maybe?" Mackenzie said with a scowl. "What do you care?"

Kalen held up his hands. "I don't."

"What's in there?" Kyla elbowed Daniel. Her chin tilted towards the bag as she peeked inside. "Goalie gloves? Let me guess. You want to play Changeball?"

"Of course!" He replied. "Don't you?"

She shrugged. "It'd be cool, but I got something much better."

She slanted her mustard-coloured bag downwards and Daniel leaned in to take a look at what she had bought. There were around ten little spheres, each a different size and colour, though they weren't very different. You could tell that there were similarities between each one.

"Am I supposed to know what they are?" Daniel raised an eyebrow.

"Are those the new collection of holograms?" Mackenzie

had leaned in now, her big eyes widening and her lips getting squeezed together in, what Daniel assumed was, jealousy. She got extra bitter when his sister nodded, got one of the spheres and tapped the middle of it.

"Cool." The sphere transformed. Orange light shot out of the sphere, getting diffracted into an image of a fierce cat with razor sharp claws and jagged stripes, which Daniel recognized immediately.

"A tiger." He breathed. The intricate detail was impossible to miss, and each side was portrayed to perfection.

"Yep." Kyla grinned. "Unfortunately, they come in packets, so you don't see which one you bought until you open it. I didn't get any special editions. Only the normal animals."

"I'm sure you'll get some soon." William assured her and she smiled at him.

The door opened and they all turned around. Julius came out with two bags, which he handed to both Mackenzie and Daniel.

"How'd it go?" He asked Kalen.

"Great."

"That's good to hear." He looked at Kyla. "Did you get what you wanted?"

"Yes. Thank you so much!"

"It was my pleasure." Julius replied. "Are you ready to go home?"

What Daniel was really ready for was to have his mom home and safe. But it'd take so much time and meanwhile, he had to stay positive. He nodded. When they all nodded, Julius pulled out a purple bubble and threw it in front of them, creating a portal once more and dragging the children through the darkness, leading them home...

# CHAPTER 6

# KYLA

"The rules are straight forward." Kalen explained, digging around in Mackenzie's closet.

He had asked Kyla to accompany him in a search to find all the equipment needed for Changeball and now they found themselves inside Mackenzie's enormous room, rummaging around her trunks, looking for what Kalen said was a 'Warall'- the crystal-clear ball shapeshifters used in this game. They had searched half the room, so far, but still couldn't find it, in all of Mackenzie's mess. Her room might look tidy at first but once you look in the closet you realise that she just dumps everything in there, out of sight.

"You just have to get the ball in the back of the net." Kalen continued. "Contact is allowed but not too brutal."

Kyla frowned. "So, it's basically football."

"Pretty much. But you pass with your hands, you can use your powers to turn into any animal you want, and the ball creates boosts."

"What do you mean?" She asked, opening an awfully full trunk, and preparing herself to dig her arm inside. It was full of frilly dresses, which were very dusty, probably out of use. Knowing Mackenzie, she would not wear any of the fancy clothes Kyla found inside and she couldn't necessarily blame her. They were way too glamorous- even for Kyla.

"Each power up gives the one in possession, well, extra power. For example: The speed boost." Kalen walked over to look under Makenzie's bed. "It makes the person faster."

"Can't we just change into a cheetah? They're fast."

"The ball even increases their speed."

"Wow." She tried to imagine a faster version of the gold-medal-sprinter cats, but her mind couldn't picture it. How fast would they run?

"AHA!" She turned at the shout. Kalen triumphantly held up a football-sized crystal ball, his expression unbearably smug as if to say even Mackenzie's room can't stop me! He walked towards her, spreading his arm dramatically towards the opened door.

"Shall we?"

Kyla smirked. "Race you there!"

She sprinted out the door, running as fast as she could, weaving in and out of corridors, dodging table edges and chairs, until she finally reached the back door. She passed a hand by her hair, which was braided into a tight ponytail and reached for the handle, pushing it open to find...

A large, no, massive, fear inflicting wasp. She could see the hair quivering on its abdomen, the antenna fluttering in time with its wings as the buzzing filled her ears pounding her head. She breathed heavily petrified and stared at the horror in front of her face. Two soulless black eyes stared at her as it approached, the stinger angling up towards her. She started not to breathe. She couldn't help it, the fear gripped her like a plague, refusing to let go. She couldn't hold it in any more...

She squealed.

A loud, squeaky shout that carried on for several seconds. She squeezed her eyes shut, preparing for never ending pain but it never came. Something touched her shoulder and she swatted at it aggressively, jumping on the balls of her feet, ready to run away from the beast.

"It's ok."

Kyla whipped around, her eyes landing on a familiar set of worried ice blue ones.

Kalen's.

"Sorry. I scared you."

She was too freaked out to catch what he said, scared that if she spoke the monster would attack, sting her repeatedly, not letting her breathe, not letting her resist or fight back...

"I'm so sorry." He repeated, grabbing her by the shoulders until her eyes met his. "I shouldn't have done that."

She let out a breath she hadn't noticed she was holding. "What?"

"I shouldn't have flown out of the window and startled you like that."

Kyla couldn't believe what she was hearing. "Wait. You were the wasp?"

"You..."

"I know. I'm so sorry." He said again, his eyes filled with concern. "I'm so competitive that I wasn't thinking straight. I just wanted to beat you to the yard, and I didn't notice you were afraid of wasps."

Her cheeks flamed with embarrassment, but she was too busy fuming. Too busy trying to find the right words of shock and fury but no words seemed to be enough, so she settled for two words.

"You cheated!"

"Actually, you never said we couldn't transform." Kalen reminded her.

Her anger stopped. He was right. She hadn't said any rules, but the idea of shapeshifting felt so new to her that she hadn't thought of it. But of course, shapeshifting must feel natural for someone like Kalen, who had lived here all his life.

"So, are you ok?" Kalen looked at her shyly as if scared of her lashing out at him, but she didn't. She felt ashamed of her behaviour and kept looking at the ground, wishing that it would just crack open and swallow her whole but her wish wasn't granted and so she was left to nod. Keeping her head facing downwards, she pulled her hair over her face, trying to hide from view as she nodded.

Kalen nodded too and they both didn't seem to know what to say after that, so decided to walk in silence over the pasture of evergreen grass. The heat beat down on them as they transformed into a pair of puppies, running towards the patch of grass at the end of the yard. Running around like a puppy felt exhilarating and Kyla wanted to keep going, racing up and down the hills, rolling around in the mud. But she saw her brother by a goal post and decided to change back.

"There you are!" Mackenzie raced towards her, whilst Kalen transformed behind them. He pulled out the Warall and handed it to Mackenzie, who scowled. "What took you so long?"

"Have you seen your room?" He replied with a roll of his eyes. "It's like all your mess threw up in your closet."

Mackenzie blushed. "I was looking for something."

"I'm sure you were."

"You don't believe me?" She countered.

"I can't say I do."

"You can believe what you want."

"I didn't realise I needed your permission."


Kyla walked between them, choosing to stay away from the argument that was brewing and wanting to go to talk to her brother, who stood at the far end.

"Hey" Daniel said, sitting on the grass and patting the space next to him, inviting Kyla to join him.

She accepted the invitation and sat on the grass, legs crossed, staring at the clear blue sky, and wondering once again about their mom. Every night she had nightmares of all the horrible things that must be happening to Cassie. All the dark walls and dungeons and constant torture. Kyla shuddered just thinking about it. She hadn't told anyone about her dreams- not even her twin, too afraid of them pitying her and assuring her that everything would be ok. She wasn't so sure. Her lips were cut from all the nervous chewing, and her nails were short from the fidgeting but she couldn't help herself.

"What's wrong?" Daniel asked her.

"Nothing."

"That would be a lot more believable if you weren't chewing your lips off, like you do when you're worried." He raised his eyebrows, pointing to where her teeth were sinking into her lips, leaving very deep dent marks. "Don't think I haven't noticed."

She sighed. Her brother knew her too well and she knew she couldn't shield her fears anymore. "I have something to tell you."

And so, she told him. Everything. From her deepest worries for their mom, to her never-ending nightmares as well as some of the sleepless nights she had spent pacing around her room, hoping that her horrifying dreams would calm down and vanish. Unfortunately, that never happened, and Kyla was left tossing and turning, wrapping her arms around herself and pulling the blankets around her head hoping it would block out the frightening scenes, but it only seemed to make her sweat from head to toes.

"I should've guessed." Daniel said, once Kyla had finished retelling every detail. He passed a hand through his hair, rumpling it up. "You're not alone."

"You can't sleep either?" Kyla felt shocked and slightly hurt. "Why didn't you tell me?"

"Same reason you didn't tell me." He replied with a shrug. "I didn't want to worry you."

Kyla looked down at her lap, ashamed of shutting her brother out, now knowing that he suffered in the same way she did.

"I miss her." Daniel whispered.

He could've meant anyone, but Kyla knew exactly who he was thinking about, and she looked at his grief-struck eyes, reaching for his hand. She twined her fingers with his, thankful that she wasn't alone.

"Me too." She said sadly. She cleared her throat and forced a smile. "So, what have you been up to? Practising for Changeball?"

"You could say that." Daniel replied. "It was mostly Mackenzie throwing random things at me to see if I could catch them. She even threw a bush once."

Suddenly, the gush on his forehead made sense as well as all the cuts and bruises running down his skinny arms. Kyla decided not to ask for details, afraid of all the things Mackenzie must've thrown towards her brother.

"Did you find the Warall?" Daniel asked and Kyla's mind flashed to Kalen as a wasp. She trembled as she told her brother about their search in Mackenzie's room and the fright that Kalen had given her.

She expected him to laugh at her fear, but he simply looked at her. "Are you ok?"

He knew how much she hated the animal. Her nod must not have been convincing because he kept assuring her that wasps weren't as bad as she thought, and that the stings barely stung but that didn't stop her from freaking out and flinching at the memory.

"It's fine." Her brother assured her. "Everyone is scared of something."

She turned towards him. "What's your fear?"

He stayed silent, then changed the subject. "Where are Mackenzie and Kalen?"

Kyla decided to leave her brother's fear a mystery- for now. "Probably still arguing."

"Nope." Mackenzie sauntered over to where they sat. Her hair was pulled back into a high ponytail and she looked fierce in her dark green leggings and black crop top. "We've actually been setting up the posts, while you two sat here doing nothing, staring at the pretty little sky as if you'd never seen it before."

"Ignore her." Kalen whispered, then he met Kyla's eyes and he apologised again for the wasp incident.

"It's ok." She assured him.

"Let's play then." Makenzie said. She looked at Kyla, eyeing her from head to toe, her eyes resting on her high boots. "You might want to change. But first let's pick the teams. I call Kyla for my team."

She looped her arm through Kyla's, dragging her to where she stood as if drawing an invisible line between them and the boys.

Kalen grinned. "I guess I'm with Daniel." He raised his hand for a high five and Daniel reluctantly obliged.

"Wait." Kyla protested. "That's not fair. They get a goalie?"

"We can play attack against defence." Mackenzie suggested then her eyes shone. "That's actually perfect. Kalen plays defence and I normally play as a full-on attacker."

"What about me?" Kyla couldn't help feeling a bit excluded: everyone knew their roles except for her.

"You can play centre." Kalen said. "You attack and

defend. Think of it like a midfielder in football."

'How come you guys know about football? Is there a league in Ocelia?" Daniel asked.

"No but that doesn't mean we don't appreciate Earth culture and watch it occasionally. It's just that the majority of shapeshifters hate humans so it's not really celebrated or played here" Kalen replied as he walked towards the goals.

"Why do shapeshifters hate humans?"

"Who cares, we have a game to win! Hurry up Kyla!" Mackenzie interrupted strolling past.

Kyla left the others, taking Mackenzie's advice and changing into some black leggings and a pink crop shirt, with short sleeves. White trainers also awaited her when she walked back out onto the field and met Mackenzie, who told her to hurry up and run a few laps to warm up. Kyla did as she was told and by the end of it, she felt warm and ready to play, all the blood of her body pumping with enthusiasm.

Once she went to Mackenzie's side of the pitch, she was met by William, his hair gelled back, a whistle tied around his neck and a smile plastered on his lips. He grinned at her.

"Good thing you changed." He whispered into her ear. "Kalen and Mackenzie can get a little competitive."

"Yeah, well so can I." Kyla smirked, yanking the whistle

from around his neck and holding it as bait. "You know which team should win don't you?"

He laughed and snatched the whistle back. "Are you trying to trick the referee into letting your team win?"

"No." she said. She leaned in close enough to whisper. "Did it work?"

"You really are competitive."

An arm wrapped around Kyla's shoulder, leading her towards the middle of the arena of grass before she could reply. Mackenzie looked back at William, probably making sure he was out of ear shot.

"Did you convince him?"

"No." Kyla shrugged.

"Oh well." She sighed, then her expression turned steely. "We need to win."

Kyla agreed and determination flowed through her, which only increased as she saw Daniel's smug expression and little mocking dance by the goal posts.

Oh, it was so on.

William blew the whistle, and the game began.

***

1 hour later and they were still hyped over the game. Julius had come home to a very chatty and wild dinner where everyone was feeling extremely smug and proud of themselves. He had to take in a lot of information including: 1. Kalen had 'accidentally' collided with Mackenzie's foot or as she claimed "had run straight into it for no reason or provocation", 2. Daniel and Kyla were actually pretty good and they believed that they could make the team, 3. Daniel had somehow managed to slip on his shoelace but still saved Mackenzie's shot with his back (He claimed it was on purpose while the girls said that he had been so concussed and confused that he had turned around to watch some ducks at the pond) 4. that William made the worst referee as he made decisions that both teams were unhappy with. And 5 that Mackenzie had again 'accidentally' kicked the ball at Kalen's head. 'His abnormally large head got in the way of my shot' she insisted.

Julius smiled. "Sounds like you had fun."

"Where did you go dad?" Mackenzie asked, whilst gobbling up her lava cake.

Kyla took a spoonful of hers, feeling the ice cream melt in her mouth and mix perfectly with the delicious chocolate flavour.

"I went to Woodford." He replied. "It appears that they have finally chosen the students in each dorm."

Kyla felt her stomach shift with nerves. Everyone at the school would have a roommate and she really hoped hers would be someone nice, funny, outgoing but also hard working. On the other hand, she could imagine her brother wanting some expert troublemaker with plenty of lists full of horrible pranks, which would surely end him in detention. She wrung her hands, twisting her fingers so much it looked as if they would snap off.

"Kyla." Julius' eyes shifted to her. "Your roommate is… Mackenzie."

"YES!" Mackenzie shrieked, dropping her spoon, and holding out her hand for a high five. Kyla was too busy sighing with relief, not believing her luck.

"Seriously?" She laughed happily, finally high-fiving Mackenzie.

"Poor you." Kalen whispered next to her. "Mackenzie as a roommate can only be described as one word: Di-sas-trous".

Mackenzie glowered at him.

"Moving on." Julius said, moving his focus onto Daniel, who tried to look confident and relaxed but failed miserably.

"Daniel, your roommate is..."

Everyone seemed to hold their breaths.

"Kalen."

"Woohoo!" Kalen celebrated. "Team KD, let's go!" He raised his hand for a high five and Daniel lifted his towards Kalen's, changing it at the last second and slapping him hard on the forehead.

"Ow!" Kalen complained, rubbing his temples. "I told you not to do that."

"I told you not to call ourselves team KD. If anything, it should be DK."

"Everyone seems happy." Julius observed, as they all finished their meals.

He grinned, then stood up from the table. "Kalen, William, you should go back home. Mackenzie, Kyla, Daniel, you should go to bed. Tomorrow is going to be a busy and exhausting day."

That was a massive understatement because tomorrow, they started... school.

# CHAPTER 7

# DANIEL

"Daniel! Come on, it's time to go!"

Daniel stumbled over a pile of clothes as he hurried to grab the slick blue suit Julius had ironed for him and close his lately packed suitcase. He had completely forgotten to pack all his things the day before, because of all the excitement of his first Changeball game- which had been a huge success. Straightening himself, he slammed his suitcase closed and went over to the bathroom right around the corner, checking his hair until it was perfectly messed up, then grabbing his suitcase and dragging it out into the corridor. After about a minute of forcing his way down the stairs, he finally made it and found his sister already dressed in a black sleeveless top and a black and red chequered, short skirt, with her arms crossed over her chest. Her black boots tapped the floor impatiently.

"About time." Kyla muttered with a smirk and then lent him a hand with his luggage, leading him outside. There he found Mackenzie, who also decided to wear a purple chequered skirt. But she had chosen to wear it with a white, long-sleeved top instead.

Shivering in the early-5am breeze, Daniel considered it a great choice and he wrapped his arms around himself.

"Give me your suitcases." Julius ordered, stepping out of the house, and Daniel handed his over, followed by Kyla. Julius threw a grey bubble, opening a circle of light, in which he dropped the suitcases. "Ready to go?" He asked, straightening up as the portal closed.

Kyla nodded and Daniel tried to, but he had to stifle a yawn instead. "Remind me why we had to wake up so early if we're teleporting there?"

Julius rumpled up his hair and Daniel frowned thinking of the minutes he had spent styling it. "It's better to be early than sorry."

"The saying is it's better to be safe than sorry." Mackenzie corrected.

Julius smiled. "This is my version."

Dead silence followed disturbed only by the chirping of

crickets as no one seemed to want to tell Julius the hard truth. His saying sucked.

Kyla was quick to change the subject. "Aren't we leaving?" She shivered in the cold, then decided to do something about it and transformed into a small arctic fox. Daniel copied her, turning into a polar bear with sharp claws and teeth, which immediately blocked the cold air and stopped his chattering teeth from crashing into each other.

"Of course." Julius took out another bubble from his pocket- multi coloured this time. "This is the school's special portal, which will take us directly inside." He explained. "Are you ready?"

They nodded; telling him that they had been ready from the moment they'd stepped out the door. Julius launched the sphere into the air, casting a rainbow swirl and leading the children towards it and their new school.

***

As Daniel stepped out of the shimmering blur, he gasped at the towering sight before him. The school was built like a castle with many wings and towers. It was huge yet omitted a friendly and calming aura. He could see some students being welcomed by all sorts of people. Talking animals stood introducing themselves as well as actual teachers who shook the student's hands. Soon the glittering entrance was shining with pride as several students bustled away from their saddened parents and towards the front door, into the building.

Daniel felt a soft touch on his shoulder, and he spun to see his sister's enthusiastic grin and glistening eyes. Kyla loved school. She loved textbooks and tests and homework and harsh teachers. She loved it all. He, on the other hand, did not love it. At all.

"Wow." Mackenzie said, impressed and something told Daniel that she was rarely awestruck.

Julius spread his arms. "Welcome to your new school."

A buzzing sound erupted from inside his jacket and Julius seized a metal stick, which he held up to his ear. "Hello? Kalen?... You're here?" He glanced at the children. "We are right in front of the north entrance. See you soon."

"I guess this is my cue to leave." Mackenzie said with a salute to her dad. She turned to leave but Julius grabbed her by the arm and pulled her into a hug. A stab of grief tore Daniel's heart apart at not being able to hug his mom, but he fought against the oncoming tears. Kyla's eyes turned glassy, and she walked over, lacing her fingers through his and holding on tight. Very tight. So tight that his hand started going numb.

He didn't want to say anything and luckily, he didn't have to as a voice called "Kyla! Daniel!", making Mackenzie glare at her father and whisper something that sounded very much like "evil genius". Kyla let go of Daniel's hand, rushing to meet Kalen.

Kalen's hair was gelled back making his ice blue strands stand out as well as the colour of his eyes. He wore a long-sleeved suit shirt, navy trousers and...

"Dude. Are you wearing a tie?" Daniel asked as Mackenzie howled with laughter.

Kalen's face burned.

"Hey, I like it." Kyla argued, shooting her brother a glare that said be nice. "It makes him look serious and mature."

She winked, hardly containing her laughter and Kalen's face burned brighter.

"Kalen, I think you look smart." Julius praised him.

Before Kalen could respond, an unfamiliar voice spoke.

"Is this the Reyhan family?"

Daniel turned around and his eyes met a pair of dazzling purple eyes, surrounded by a similar shade of eye shadow. The girl in front of them looked about 16 years old, with long dynamite coloured hair that curled at the ends and contained violet purple streaks, a similar colour to her eyes. She wore a white top over her caramel-coloured skin, jeans and a denim vest which had a clip that read 'Rhea'.

"Yes, this is my daughter." Julius said, introducing Mackenzie to the girl. "And these are Kalen, Kyla and Daniel."

"Perfect. Surprisingly, you're all on my list." She smiled, looking up from her clipboard. "I'm Rhea. I will be your guide to your dorm rooms." She held out her hand to Mackenzie, then Kalen, Kyla and finally to Daniel, who shook it as well. Her grip was strong, firm and Daniel made his the same, releasing it only when Rhea released her hold.

"I can take it from here." She told Julius and he smiled, taking out a bubble out of his pocket and throwing it in front of him.

"Thank you." He stepped into the light and the next second he was gone.

"Follow me." Rhea gestured towards the winding stairs and Daniel followed her intrigued and anxious to discover everything he could. His eyes largened with every step as he took in the sheer enormity and beauty being radiated off this empowering structure. The entire construction and walls appeared to be made from opals which created a unique and impressive product. Rhea explained how centuries ago a powerful shapeshifter had managed to transform a normal human based castle into the school, transforming the entire building so that it would be made of beautiful opals. She also said that the shapeshifter had managed to create changing rooms which were able to customise themselves depending on the user's tastes. However, when asked whether the dorm rooms would be like this impressive view, she just winked and said that all would be revealed. This had the desired effect and instantly Daniel was twitching with excitement.

At last, they reached their dorms and Daniel could see that his friends were just as ecstatic as he was. The only thing in the way was a huge stone wall, which rose several feet off the ground. Rhea stopped and turned towards them, her eyes serious now.

"Ok, here are the keys to your room. You each get one set so don't lose them! They control everything in the house, so they are very valuable. You have one hour to start customising your rooms and exploring the house, so have fun! Daniel, Kalen, you're the house on the left Kyla, Mackenzie, yours is a little further on and behind their one so I'll have to take you to it".

Daniel was confused. A house? Did she mean the castle as a house? He was just about to ask when Rhea tapped one of the curves on the stone and the door swung open, answering all the questions that flowed in his mind. In the yard there were... houses. Large cottages littered the place, and he felt his mouth drop. Beside him Kalen's eyes had widened so much he looked like an alien. Turning around Daniel swiped the keys to the house and sprinted ahead, leaving Rhea incredibly confused and Kalen gaping. He could see Mackenzie turn and do the same thing and they just had time to give each other a high five before they turned and reached their homes. His hands shaking a little, he inserted the key into the lock and swung the door open, rushing inside to check out his new home, which was...

Blank.

What?

He ran around inspecting every room and all the walls. There was nothing. No furniture, no wallpaper, nothing. Not even stairs for the upper levels. He was scratching his head when Kalen burst through. Daniel turned and was about to ask what was wrong when Kalen spoke in a smug voice.

"I know what to do."

"Oh, do you now?" Daniel said sarcastically, turning his back on Kalen.

"I found the instruction manual!" Daniel whipped around, his eyes stopping on the little booklet clasped in Kalen's hand and his triumphant smile as he held it just out of Daniel's reach. Even on his tippy toes, Daniel couldn't reach it as Kalen held it above his head.

Kalen flipped through it mumbling as he passed the pages. "Yes. Aha. Mmm."

"Can I see?" Daniel asked.

"What's the magic word?"

"Abracadabra duh!" Daniel said, looking at Kalen as if he was an idiot. Kalen glared at him, but Daniel stole the manual from him before he could react, leaving Kalen muttering something along the lines of "Abracadabra hmph hilarious. I'm Daniel and I think …" Luckily Daniel avoided hearing the end of his epic rant as he began customising their new pad with Kalen sullenly following alongside him, doing what could best be described as 'sulking'.

45 minutes later Daniel looked on at his new home with pride. Together he and Kalen had managed to turn this once barren space into an incredible living area. The living room had been transformed to contain a massive Tv screen, one red

couch, a beanbag chair and an armchair. When Kalen questioned his decision for so many seats, Daniel simply explained that he expected Mackenzie and Kyla to visit them every day and bug them (this mostly applied to Mackenzie who he had no doubt would annoy them till the end of time). They had also added a library which connected to the living area and was filled with hundreds of books and tables to study at and at Daniel's request created a laboratory and forgery which they could work in.

Daniel had also decided to make a second floor and quick as a flash, created a set of stairs which connected both layers. Upstairs contained their separate bedrooms with Kalen's being mostly empty apart from a few posters and furniture, while Daniel's contained glass showcases where he would store his action figures and collectibles as well as having his own smaller TV connecting to Ocelia's equivalent to a PS5: a Orquazator. This was a small device which was controlled manually and included both VR and controller games. But what Daniel was most proud about was all the sports facilities they had added which included: a bowling alley, a basketball court, a tennis court, one table tennis table, a pinball machine, a 25m swimming pool and a subterranean training area where he could practise fighting against robots.

Now all that was left was the wallpaper. Kalen argued to make it all navy blue, but Daniel convinced him to turn it into a shapeshifting wallpaper which was different every day. Sometimes it would look as if they were underwater, sometimes as if they were in a rainforest or on a mountain. Overall, Daniel was feeling extremely happy with the final product when there was a knock on the door. Kalen reached it first and swung it open to find Rhea and the girls waiting for them.

"Hey guys so I have to take you to your first lesson. The school wants to let you have a first taste of all the new and exciting things that we are going to teach you and for you to start meeting the teachers. So, hurry up." She said, grabbing Kalen and Daniel and shoving them towards the corridor. Daniel could only sputter as he was dragged along to their first class which was...

Self-defence.

Oh great, Daniel had never fought anyone before and now he had to fight shapeshifters.

This was going to hurt. A lot.

Daniel hurriedly sat at the back of the pitch-black room where he hoped he would not be seen but was immediately joined by Mackenzie who was muttering something like "Why would they sit at the front? Bozos..." while staring daggers at Kyla and Kalen who (no surprise) had chosen to sit at the very front of the class. As he sat, Daniel watched a large number of other children begin to fill in the seats and talk to each other as if they were old friends. He was just starting to doze off when he heard a large thump next to him and opened an eye. A small boy with light skin and longish yellow dreadlocks with a hint of black streaks had sat next to him. The boy turned and took out a hand.

"Hi, my name is Zilef. Zilef Rascau and you are?" he said, his dark blue eyes glinting in the darkness. Daniel took his hand and shook it, impressed by the boy's strength.

"I'm Daniel Whixx. I just moved here." he said, explaining where he came from just as another boy came and flopped down next to him.

"Wait you lived on Earth dude?" said the new boy. He had long black hair which he kept out of his eyes, which were as black as the night sky. His hair contained silver streaks too and from the slump of his shoulders, Daniel could see that the boy looked incredibly bored of this class.

"I'm Delvin by the way, I've always wanted to go to a different dimension before. What was it like?" he asked, totally immersed and curious. Daniel only had time to open his mouth when the lights switched on, revealing a chair in the middle. Then they switched off again just as quickly, as a small voice filled the class.

"Stupid lights not working. How am I meant to do my dramatic entrance now? It's like this every year. I try it for so long over the holidays to impress the little rugrats but when the big moment comes it fails miserably. Every single time. It never works and now I can't even begin to frighten the little snobs waiting for me. This year is going to be a torture I bet. I bet some of them can't even punch a guy. Such a disappointment." The rant continued for a good five minutes before the voice seemed to realise everyone was waiting for him and could hear everything he had just said. The chair in the middle of the classroom suddenly turned around and Daniel could see an old man sitting there with sunglasses on and tapping a remote furiously.

"Oh, em hello there. Pleased to see you all. My name is Mr Sedgwick Smithy, and I shall unfortunately be your self-defence teacher for the year." He stopped and posed like a superhero waiting for a round of applause before being met with the uncomfortable truth. The students thought he was a joke. Huffing, he got up and started walking to the board when he tripped face first onto the ground. Suddenly

Mackenzie started howling with laughter at the poor teacher's misfortune which Daniel considered to be rather unkind, and Mr Smithy snapped his attention towards her.

"Oh, so you think it's funny do you Ms Reyhan? Oh, I'll show you something funny! Detention and I don't care whether it's the first day! You can go to detention at lunch and stay there for the entire hour." He spat, quite literally swelling with anger. No. Daniel was serious. He literally started inflating like a balloon. However, Mackenzie remained cool and looked at him innocently as she spoke.

"Oh, but Sir I wasn't laughing at your patheticness I was actually laughing at what Daniel had just told me. Oh yes, he just told me that the Jaguars are going to win the title over the Falcons. Can you believe him sir? Oh, it's just too funny. I couldn't contain myself." She said, wiping tears of laughter from her face. Luckily it appeared that Mr Smithy was a bit senile with his old age and merely mistook these tears for guilt and he smiled at her showing some perfectly white teeth and showing off the little white hairs he had left which had light charcoal coloured streaks.

"Oh yes that is funny. Ok then no detention. Now moving on." He reached up, looking as if he was about to smooth out his hair but then realised that he had very little to style and settled for grabbing a long stick, which he used to reach a kind of button on the ceiling. A whiteboard appeared behind him, and he tapped the stick against it, pointing at the words which had formed.

"My name is Mr Smithy. Not Sir Smith. Not Sir Smithity." He glared down at the students, removing his sunglasses for mere seconds to show his light, hazel eyes. "Mr Smithy."

"He really is an old bat." Mackenzie muttered under her breath at Daniel. He didn't really know what an "old bat" meant but it didn't sound like a compliment and Daniel didn't want to ask, scared of what the old man would do if he heard him talking during his lecture.

"Does everyone know what I will be teaching?" Mr Smithy asked.

No one seemed to want to raise their hands, too scared by their new teacher. Daniel could see Mr Smithy scowl until two hands were raised.

"Yes?"

"Self Defence sir!" Kyla and Kalen answered simultaneously.

"Very good. Very good. Very good." He kept muttering the words, his eyes staring at a spot on the wall as if he was lost in thought. A kid with dark skin and dark brown, almost black, spiky hair and red streaks cleared their throat and he snapped back, turning back towards the board and tapping it with his stick, much harder than before.

"There are rules in this classroom." Mr Smithy started to pace in front of the students, making Daniel a little dizzy and reminding him a lot of a predatory shark stalking its prey. He stopped walking and stared at Daniel. It felt as if he was digging into his soul and Daniel couldn't suppress his shiver as Mr Smithy said, "Which will need punishments if broken."

Daniel didn't know what it was with Shapeshifters and how they always seemed to know about his trouble making habits, but the way Mr Smithy stared at him made him incredibly itchy and fidgety, which increased as he smiled wickedly.

"Now for a demonstration in my class." The old man smiled towards the back of the class. "Ah, Ms Reyhan." Mackenzie shifted beside Daniel but managed to keep her chin raised and a look of determination on her face as Mr Smithy motioned for her to stand up. "Come. Let's show the rest of these stuck-up children a few exercises of which we will learn in the coming weeks."

Daniel could see Kyla's jaw drop as Mackenzie marched towards the middle of the class, whilst Kalen muttered something under his breath, his lips curving upwards. Mackenzie walked between rows of tables, tucking loose strands of hair behind her ears and cracking her knuckles as she came closer to the insane teacher. He motioned for her to come closer still and then raised his remote up to the ceiling.

Nothing happened.

Mr Smithy let out a string of very bad words, tapping the control impatiently. A CRACK sounded and the floor around Mackenzie and himself rose above the ground, tables, and students. Daniel heard Mackenzie's gasp even from where he sat at the opposite end of the room and noticed her slight stumble at the sudden movement of the ground. A plastic ring formed around the platform, making Daniel's eyes widen. It looked a lot like a boxing ring.

"Have you ever fought before?" Mr Smithy asked Mackenzie, his smile broadening as she shook her head. "There's a first time for everything...I guess."

Some students at the far side of the class snickered but Daniel frowned, his mind imagining all kinds of horrors to come in his friend's immediate future. His frown deepened, when Mr Smithy positioned himself in a battle stance, arms crossed in front of him.

"In the next few days, you will learn how to kick..." He thrust out his leg with an impossible speed for someone his age and slammed it into Mackenzie's gut, who toppled backwards, gasping for breath. She bounced back up seconds later, arms in front of her as she hopped from one foot, onto the other, preparing herself.

"You will learn how to punch..." He lunged forwards again and Daniel gripped his chair as Mackenzie ducked his fist. He was about to cheer when Mr Smithy launched another punch. This time Mackenzie didn't have time to move out of the way and got thrown back.

Rubbing her cheek, Mackenzie got back up rushing towards the man, jumping and kicking her leg at him only to have it caught and thrown back. "You will learn how to block attacks. Deflect attacks. And counter attacks." Mr Smithy explained. "Leaving your enemies in defeat." He pointed to where Mackenzie had hit the net around the ring. He walked towards her, turning to the class, a wicked smile on his lips. "You will have lots to learn. You will fall. You will fail. You will...OOOF!"

The old man stumbled back, his hands over his stomach, staring at the raised fist in front of him. Mackenzie cracked her knuckles. "Sorry. We didn't really catch that last sentence." She said it with a grin and Daniel leaned forward, trying to warn Mackenzie of the raging man in front of her but Mr Smithy simply laughed.

He giggled uncontrollably, rolling on the mat, clutching his heaving sides as he spoke between gasping breaths. "I... DEFINITELY... DESERVED...THAT!"

The whole class went dead silent. Daniel figured you could even hear a pin drop as he glanced at Zilef and Delvin, who were both staring at Mr Smithy half amused and appalled. Mackenzie had a similar expression on her face, and she dropped to the ground, snatching something from the middle of the ring. She pressed a button on the remote and the platform lowered, making the teacher's strange fit more visible.

Mackenzie turned towards the rows of seats but before she could escape and hide at the back of the class, like Daniel knew she wanted to, Mr Smith screamed at her. "WAIT!"

The old man stood up, looking at Mackenzie with a strange look. "I can't believe I'm saying this, but you've got guts kid." He waved Mackenzie to her seat, and she sunk into it, releasing a relieved sigh that went on for a couple of seconds. Daniel looked at her and whispered if she was ok. She smiled as she nodded.

"Well punks." Zilef nudged Daniel in the ribs and he was forced to turn his attention back to Mr Smithy, who smiled wickedly at the end of the classroom.

"It seems this year might have some surprises in store."

***

"Daniel, I think we're lost."

Kyla had muttered the words ten thousand times already, but Daniel ignored her, touching his wristband, turning it off and on again. Rhea had given everyone a holographic wristband, which contained multiple functions such as phone calls, reminders and most importantly a map of the school.

Daniel clasped the other three wristbands in his hand. Hot pink. Periwinkle. Navy. All of the ones belonging to his friends, who glared at him and whispered things like "stubborn" behind his back.

Daniel had to admit that he was acting a bit stubborn.

Only a bit.

It was not like he had decided to never give them their wristbands...only until he figured out where to go and had led them to the right classroom. After a boring lecture in Strategy class, he deserved a little fun. Professor Cecelia Pomieko, a short woman with copper coloured hair and watermelon pink streaks, hazel almond shaped eyes and a strict no lateness policy had bored Daniel to death with her long rambling of tactics and techniques. The only interesting part which Daniel had managed to pay attention to, was the idea of playing team games like capture the flag or paintball.

"Daniel..."

"Give me a minute!" He tore a hand through his hair in his stress. He could feel Kalen become more agitated by the minute and mutter "we're going to be late" continuously under his breath. Mackenzie on the other hand was strolling behind, completely at ease, not caring whatsoever if they arrived late. Like she said, "at least they would get there sometime during the day."

Daniel smacked the wristband a little harder, zooming into the red dot which marked where they stood. He scratched his head. He wasn't lost... he was just finding the quickest route. Kyla walked up to him and before Daniel could figure out what she was doing, she snatched the three wristbands from his soft grasp, flinging them towards the others. Mackenzie caught her pink one without raising her head as Kalen barely got his before it hit the ground.

"Ok. I know the way." Kyla told everyone, whilst adjusting

her periwinkle band and doing zooming in actions, trying to see the map clearer. She pointed left and Kalen raced after her whilst Mackenzie sauntered behind them, and Daniel walked beside her, scrolling down his wristband and trying to get a hang of the map.

He was so busy staring at the hologram that he didn't notice everyone else had stopped until he barged into Kyla, hurling them both tumbling to the ground.

"Ouch. Get off me! Get off me!" She cried, squeezing out from under him and standing up. She went back to where Kalen stood whilst Mackenzie helped Daniel up. They both joined the others just as the wooden door opened.

Beyond the door lay a grassy plane covered in all sorts of flowers and plants that bloomed under the illusioned sun. Mini worktables littered the area along with stools, which were already filled with students. Kyla, Mackenzie, Kalen, and Daniel eyed the spaces, searching for empty seats and Daniel's throat hurt as he let out a deafening groan. There were only five seats left empty.

At the front of the class.

Daniel hunched, keeping his head sorely on the ground and making his way to one of the seats. At the front of the class! He felt everyone's eyes on him, and he slouched lower, sinking into one of the highchairs and laying his head on the table in front of him. A screech echoed nearby, and Mackenzie slipped into the seat next to him, Kyla taking the next seat onwards beside her and Kalen sitting on Daniel's other side, already scanning the room around them. It was quite large with the walls portraying a forest landscape. The chairs and tables were of simple wood but what caught Daniel's eye was something at the front of the class. There were two giant grey tubes filled with a blue liquid. On the sides there were several syringes and Daniel could see little drawings and words on the side however they were too far away for him to make out. Suddenly, he felt something collide with the back of his head. He turned around and saw a piece of paper on the floor beside him. He scanned the room and found the person who had thrown it. It was a tall blonde boy with orange streaks and blue eyes. He had a long pointed nose which gave Daniel the impression of a blonde Pinocchio and admittedly, a much meaner one. He sneered at him and Daniel's fingers curled into a fist when Kalen gripped his shoulder.

"That's Malcom, he's a jerk. Don't engage or you'll just make it worse." Kalen muttered under his breath. Mackenzie tapped his hand to calm him down and shook her head, glaring at Malcom. Daniel sighed but listened to them, after all they knew most of the people from their old school. If they said Malcom was bad, Malcolm was bad. Out of the corner of his eyes he saw Malcom's snooty expression disappear and be replaced by one of fury when the door was thrown open and a tall woman with glasses and pink flowing hair came in. She was incredibly young with white streaks in her salmon-coloured hair. She had a girlish face and her eyes were alight with excitement.

"Good morning class my name is Ms Piper Orgi and I will be your Study of magical creatures and demon's teacher for this year. Now today I want to not only explain what we will be doing but also want you guys to do a small practical." she said. Daniel leaned forward, already excited.

"This year we will be covering all the basic types of creatures which inhabit our world and today you will get the chance to create your own hybrid with the vials provided on this table. I will be deciding on the groups and yes that is very mean of me, but I just want you guys to meet other people on your first day so who's ready to work?" She asked. An instant cheer was her response and she set about making the pairs.

"Alright Mackenzie you are with Gabbi, Lucas goes with Vazquez, Kyla you're with Zilef, Kalen with Livia, Malcom with Delvin, Daniel with Ingrid..." Daniel zoned out. Great he was with the royal lemon girl he thought sarcastically. She'll probably boss me around the whole time. He moved to one of the side tables. He waited and a small pretty girl joined him. She had midnight black hair with different colour streaks and vibrant teal eyes, which stood out in contrast with her deeply tanned skin.

"Hi, I'm Ingrid and you're Daniel, right?" she asked, smiling.

"Uh yeah that's me. It's a pleasure to meet you. I've heard a bit about you." he said, shaking her hand.

"Good or bad?" she replied, her teal eyes sparkling. Daniel now felt rather guilty and thought perhaps he had judged her rather hastily.

"Hey, I like your hair, that's pretty cool having different coloured streaks." he said pointing. Ingrid blushed but looked pleased.

"Thanks, I got it from my mom's side of the family. So, do you have any ideas on the creature you want to make? I think we should divide the choices. Miss Orgi said we can put 4 different animal's DNA so let's each pick 2 since that's the fairest thing to do. What do you think?" she said hurriedly.

"Ok sure. I was thinking maybe bat and panda since that could be really cool and cute at the same time." Daniel replied, inspecting all the DNA samples. There were so many suddenly available on the desks of each table as if they had appeared out of thin air.

Ingrid grabbed the two vials which Daniel had suggested, smiling up at him. "Cool. I want some dinosaurs. How about an Ankylosaurus and a Spinosaurus?"

Daniel beamed. It looked like he would have a lot of fun with this girl, and they set off looking around at other tables for the dinosaur DNA samples. Daniel made his way over to where Kyla was talking to Zilef, who kept nodding at what she was saying.

"Maybe we could also do dragon and cheetah, since they are super cool animals." She was saying as Daniel approached.

"Yeah." Zilef agreed. "Fire breathing and insanely fast. I like it."

Kyla beamed at the praise and noticed Daniel next to her. She grinned. "How's it going with Ingrid?"

"Better than I thought." He replied, his face heating with shame.

"That's great!" Kyla patted him on the back, then turned back to look for some DNA vials.

Zilef leaned into Daniel. "Your sister is so cool!"

Daniel frowned. "Are we talking about the same person?" He smiled and elbowed Zilef. "Just kidding! She is pretty awesome. I'm guessing you and Kyla are getting along then?"

"Yep. You ok with Ms Princess over there?" Zilef tilted his chin to where Ingrid was busy talking to Mackenzie's partner. Gabbi, a girl with blond hair and moss green streaks. Her height made Ingrid look like a five-year-old as she towered over the smaller girl, her tall frame shadowing everyone around her. The girl's honey brown eyes suddenly turned towards Daniel and she smiled. He smiled back, choosing to go back to their table and wait for Ingrid to join him. He waved at Zilef and walked to the side of the class.

"Excuse me everyone." Ms Orgi shouted over the noise. "Does anyone have the raptor DNA?" She waited to look around the room. No one seemed to find any samples. "I swear I put out like 10 of them. Oh well." She turned to Kalen, who stood beside her. "I'll see if I can get my hands on one more sample."

That's odd. Daniel thought but before he could dwell on it, Ingrid sat down beside him, holding some vials up to his face.

"Found them!" She said with a grin. "Shall we get to work

Dr Whixx?" She pulled her hair back into a ponytail and held out some gloves to Daniel, who leaned in and took them from her, slipping them over his fingers and pulling on some protective goggles before turning back to her.

"We shall."

They dived right in, opening the holographic screen, and scanning through the different DNA adjustment selections. Daniel leaned forward in his seat as Ingrid scrolled down, modifying the DNA, and styling the animal. She was midway through another page before she paused suddenly and turned to Daniel.

"Shouldn't we sketch what we want it to look like first?"

Daniel pondered her question, mentally smacking himself for not being the one to think of it as he nodded. He opened one of the table drawers and dug around for a pencil and piece of paper.

"Ok." He said, biting his lip. "I was thinking..."

*** 

Rhea stood waiting for them as Daniel and his friends crossed the grass field towards their huts after a long exhausting day of lessons. He barely had the energy to stand up, much less to walk all the way back to their house after the boring lesson they had just been through.

Theoretical shapeshifting was one tedious lecture after another as the tall, black haired with blood red streaks teacher told them all about the lessons to come. Monsieur Pris kept rambling on and on, and Daniel felt his consciousness slip away in the passing seconds but luckily Mackenzie was there to slap him hard on the arm and he was able to at least look like he was paying attention. Honestly? Everyone looked on the verge of sleep apart from Kyla, Kalen and Ingrid, who leaned forward, their eyes glued to the teacher.

Daniel unfortunately spent the whole time worrying about their mother. What if she was hurt? What if she was trapped forever? What if she was…

Someone tapped Daniel's shoulder and he snapped back to the present.

"I was asking how your classes were?" Rhea tilted her head at him, and he shrugged, not wanting to waste his breath.

Kyla on the other hand went through the whole day, telling Rhea all about the classes, new friends and especially about the magical creatures' project.

"It was pretty exhausting actually." She concluded and everyone nodded their agreement. "I'm glad we can relax now."

"Yeah..." Rhea said.

"What?" Daniel asked because the 'yeah' she just spoke wasn't the kind of 'you're totally right' yeah.

It was more of a 'the thing is…' yeah, which got followed by horrible news. Daniel's heart rate increased, and he saw Mackenzie wring her hands tightly.

"You know what?" Rhea said. "Go get changed into your jump suit and meet me outside."

Kalen shook his head. "No. You've got us all intrigued now so how about you tell us what we need to do?"

"How do you know you have to do something?" Rhea asked, impressed.

Kalen laughed. "Please." He scoffed. "My mom's the principal, I think I know how to find out certain things."

Rhea raised an eyebrow but didn't ask further. "Ok."

Daniel waited for her to say something else, but she didn't. After several minutes she laughed.

"You guys should see your faces." Everyone glowered at her and she held up her hands in surrender. "Ok. Ok."

Rhea turned and Daniel thought she was going to lead them somewhere, but she simply pointed to the back of her shirt. Covering the whole back was a white, tentacular creature, its tentacles reaching out to the edges of the shirt and sweeping through to the edges of the front side. It had purple designs, the same colour as the shirt itself and left a cool 3D effect.

"Is that an octopus?" Kyla asked, confused.

Rhea nodded. "It's my house logo. I'm an Optimistic Octopus." Everyone cringed at the name. "I know. I'm trying my best to change it. To be fair all the names are a bit weird, and our captain is a downright moron."

"What house are we in?" Kyla and Mackenzie asked simultaneously but Daniel already knew where this conversation was going, and he felt himself groan.

Rhea turned around to face them, her face untranslatable as she looked each of them in the eye. Daniel turned, with a worried look towards his friends as Rhea spoke the five nerve-racking words that followed.

"We're about to find out".

# CHAPTER 8

# KYLA

"Kyla Whixx, please enter the arena."

The voice blared over the excited whispers coming from behind the entrance, where several students, including Kyla, paced anxiously before their allocated time. Kalen, Daniel, and Mackenzie had all already gone inside and been tested but Kyla remained walking around, hoping to tire out the stress presently burning inside of her.

She bit her lip, wrung her hands so tight they started going numb and twirled her hair around her finger so many times that it, too, had gone senseless, leaving her with the urge to bite off all her nails and pull out several strands of her hair from her high ponytail. Kyla passed her hand over the sleek jumpsuit and glanced at the patch on her shoulder, scared to see which colour it would turn.

From what she had heard, the Crocodiles were the worst house, and she really didn't want to end up in a bad house. Then again, she had only heard this fact from Rhea, who as an Octopus, greatly disliked all other houses for no apparent reason whatsoever. She had been begging them consistently to get into the Optimistic Octopuses and Kyla did like the house shirt more than all the other ones. Apparently, they had to wear the shirt to every class (except practical shapeshifting and self-defence) to show some house spirit and Kyla flinched thinking about how she'd look wearing the other house shirts. Purple was definitely her preferred colour.

Her train of thoughts stopped as another call blasted out of the speakers, making every student around her turn to stare in her direction. Keeping her head down and trying to hide behind her fringe, Kyla bustled through the door and into the arena to find...

Complete darkness.

Wait.

The door slammed closed in her face and she was forced to turn back to the room, squinting in the darkness until she realised that she could transform into a nocturnal animal. Black wings sprung from her arms, and she leapt into the air as a fruit bat, batting her arms to stay adrift as her eyesight cleared and the darkness disappeared, revealing a maze, filled with perilous obstacles.

Spiky logs spun over a sea filled with what looked like electric eels. Rocks hung on the walls as well as ropes which dangled from above but what frightened Kyla the most was the bright red count down and the beeping that echoed around her. The blaring noise which reminded her far too much of the attack on her house a few days back. The attack where her mom had been taken from her.

Kyla shook her head, clearing the painful flashbacks from her mind and storing them somewhere far in her mind to worry about later. She was sure they would revisit her in her nightmares but for now she had to use all her energy to get through this. To complete the obstacles. To ace the test.

Her eyes scanned each obstacle course, realising one thing. There were hardly any obstacles in the sky and those that were challenging would greatly ignore small creatures so a plan started forming in her head and she focused in on it but the more she thought, the more it felt like she was missing something crucial.

She looked up. The gaps in the sky were far too small for a bird to pass through. Her heart sank as the reality of failing the test became clearer unless...

Kyla stopped.

Unless...

She was a shapeshifter. She could morph into any creature so what if she turned into something that could fly and was incredibly smaller than a bird? She concentrated, gathering her thoughts and imagining her shape getting smaller and shorter and wings sprouting from her back. She felt a tingling sensation and looked at her body. She was a dragonfly!

A really small dragonfly, which could easily fit through the wavering obstacles. But she didn't have time to marvel at her success. She had to race through the maze.

As quick as she could go, Kyla flew across the room, her wings beating with energy, and to the finish line with relative ease. As soon as her wings passed the red line, the beeping stopped, and the room went quiet. A door opened to her left and she quickly transformed to her normal self before entering a large outside area. She saw her friends in the middle and dropped down next to Gabbi and the darker skinned boy with black and red hair who had snapped Mr Smithy back into the present during their earlier class. He nodded and introduced himself as Vasquez while all around the table people were chatting and talking. Kyla tried to focus as she met some new people, Lucas and Livia, but she wasn't really listening. She was way too nervous about the test outcomes yet to come. She was so nervous that she wouldn't even touch her food, much less hear what her friends were discussing.

The only thing she did notice was when suddenly Kalen's mom walked up and the whole area went silent. As everyone turned and sat up straighter, Kyla could now see that the field was split into three areas- purple, green and blue.

"Good afternoon, everyone!" She beamed, her cobalt eyes glistening in the sunlight. Kyla's head snapped up and she sat forward.

"Good afternoon," everyone replied as Kalen's mothers stepped forward. In her hands were flames of purple, blue and green: the colours of the houses. The flames licked her hand as they fought each other to be the most prominent one. She stepped forward and waited as Ms Pomieko stepped up with a roll of paper.

"When you are called, walk up to Ms Smith and allow her to place the fire into your sleeve patch. The flames will decide your house and after that you are to move over to sit with them for the evening as us teachers will explain what the first yearly challenge is."

"Now first off Zilef!" she called.

Zilef rose from his seat and made his way to Ms Smith's

side. She smiled and placed the fire onto his sleeve. Before Kyla's eyes the patch on his shoulder turned a beautiful dark blue and an illusion of the head of an ox floated above him. A cheer rose from the blue side and Zilef joined them where he was met with high fives and fist bumps.

"Arnold!" Ms Pomieko called and again, the boy's suit turned dark blue.

"Malcom!" Kyla 's eyes stared around as the blonde boy moved up to the flames and in no time, his sleeve turned green, and a snapping crocodile appeared above him. Delvin, Livia and Vazquez also became part of the ox house while Malcom's cronies Bruzo, Dane and two girls, Zila and Aina, became crocodiles.

"Ingrid!" Daniel cheered encouragingly and the small girl moved up to Kalen's mom. This time her shoulder patch became purple and a giant tentacled creature materialised above her. Kyla watched as Kalen and Mackenzie joined her in the middle of the room. Now it was Kyla's turn. Her palms were so sweaty it was as if she had washed them with water for ten minutes. She was suddenly glad that no one was near her as she approached the beautiful flames. She watched as the fire reached her shoulder and then the world went black...

She was standing in a pitch-black area. She stood and

turned around. There were three lights coming from behind and as she looked, she could see three different doorways waiting for her. Each one was unique and different in their own way. The first was a malevolent red colour pulsing with power. The middle a calm sandy yellow while the third was a clear white colour with fine mist blowing out from it. She looked at the first door and was met with a crushing sensation as if the entire world had given its power to her and she stepped back, gasping and panting. She shook her head and moved to the far left one. A chill ran down her spine and she could hear the whispers of those who had attacked them and the beeping from the attack on their house filled the air. She backed away as her mother's screams echoed in her ears. The final one gave no sounds or feelings, only a gentle calming sensation. Kyla breathed in and stepped through it.

Suddenly she was back in front of Gwenda and as she glanced at her shoulder, she realised that it had changed, now inked with an octopus surrounded by purple. She looked around confused and met Ingrid's eyes. Ingrid shook her head and motioned for her to come. Her feet weighing down heavily on her, Kyla flopped down next to Ingrid and continued to watch the ceremony.

"What happened?" Kyla asked her shakily, careful to

whisper the words so that only Ingrid heard her.

"It's OK, Kyla, that's just how we're chosen." Ingrid told her, patting her on the back. "The flames are meant to show you those doors. It means that they want you but that you must make the final decision. So, to make you choose the right option they give you samples of each house. It is said that each individual is meant to react differently based on their subconsciousness and whether or not they deserve to be there."

"Oh."

"Kyla!" She turned and found Daniel, Mackenzie and Kalen all racing towards her, pointing at the sleeves on their suits and squeaking with joy.

"We're all in the same house!" Daniel exclaimed, smiling at Ingrid.

"Why is that by the way?" Mackenzie frowned.

"What do you mean?" Kalen asked, rolling his eyes.

"How come, out of all the houses, we coincidentally end up in the same one?"

Kyla nodded. Mackenzie made a fair point.

"GUYS!" Everyone turned and racing towards them was Rhea, a huge smile plastered on her lips, her purple eyes ever so vibrant. She shrieked, hugging them all in turn and leaving

Kyla looking at a very awkward Ingrid, who obviously had no idea who Rhea was and presently viewed her as an older stranger, who hugged randomly.

Rhea stepped back after hugging Kyla, lifting her hair over her shoulders. "I can't believe you're all Optimistic Octopuses." Ingrid cringed, whilst everyone else's eyes just twitched.

"I take it you've had no luck changing the name?" Kyla asked Rhea, remembering her earlier statement of changing the name. Rhea shook her head, then dug around in her bag, which was hung over one shoulder.

"I almost forgot the reason I came here." She took out five purple shirts; the same type she was wearing with tentacles at the sides and a white octopus at the back, handing one to each of Kyla's friends before giving her one.

Kyla unfolded it, pressing it against her chest to check the size, then figuring out that it was customizable and could shrink or grow to fit the person wearing it. Her eyes followed the design, marvelling at the intricate details she could now see up close. The octopus really did look 3D.

"Anyway." Rhea stopped. She turned shamefully to Ingrid. "I'm so sorry. I'm so rude! My name is Rhea, I'm a third-year student. What's your name?"

"Ingrid."

"I love your hair." Ingrid blushed. Rhea was about to leave when a light bulb seemed to switch on in her mind. "Wait. Are you Ingrid Lemoine?"

Ingrid reluctantly nodded and Rhea gasped. "INGRID LEMOINE IS IN MY HOUSE? MY HOUSE?"

Ingrid flinched, turning around nervously. Several heads had snapped towards them, and certain students whispered excitedly.

"Can you not shout it so the whole world can hear?" Ingrid snapped.

"Sorry." Rhea whispered and hung her head. "I can't believe you're in the same school as me, much less that you're actually talking to ME! Sorry. I need to go call my parents." She skipped off before Kyla could figure out what just happened.

Like, what just happened?

"Well, that was weird." Daniel said after a long pause and Kyla had to agree. "What was that about?"

Mackenzie elbowed him in the ribs, and he managed to cover part of his wince, but Ingrid noticed. "It's ok." She spoke. "My family is just kind of famous."

"We know you're royalty." Kyla told her. Daniel,

Mackenzie, and Kalen nodded in agreement and Ingrid flushed, pulling her hair in front of her face, probably in an attempt to hide her blushing cheeks.

She looked at Daniel. "If you knew, why did you act so normal towards me?"

He shrugged. "Why wouldn't I?"

"Because..."

When she didn't continue Daniel stepped in. "Because you're royalty?"

"Well yeah."

"So, you thought we would treat you differently because your family is important?" Kyla asked, shaking her head when Ingrid nodded.

"That's the stupidest thing I've ever heard!" Daniel said appalled. "And I live with her!"

"HEY!" Kyla swatted him hard on the arm as soon as he pointed at her, then turned back to Ingrid. "He's right though. The fact that your mom is the queen doesn't change who you are and so it shouldn't change how people treat you."

"Yeah." Mackenzie and Kalen said simultaneously.

Ingrid looked up, her teal eyes shining with unshed tears. "Thanks."

"No problem." Kyla smiled. Her wrist shook a bit and a

hushed beep alerted her to her incoming messages on her wristwatch. She swiped up. "Looks like we have the next few hours to relax. Apparently, it's lights out at 10:00."

"Want to explore?" Ingrid suggested. "We can change out of our suits and into these shirts." She held up her purple house shirt.

"Sounds good." Kalen said with a smirk. "Meet at Mackenzie's and Kyla's place? Is that, ok?" He looked at both girls who smiled and agreed, saying to meet at around 7:30 and walking through the field towards their hut.

The whole walk, Kyla couldn't help feeling sorry for Ingrid. It must've been hard growing up, knowing that people might use her because of her family name. She kept thinking about all the pressure her friend must feel, even after she had changed into her house shirt and a purple skirt. However, she soon put it out of her mind as the doorbell rang and she made her way down to find Kalen, Daniel and Ingrid all changed and wearing their house shirts. Mackenzie came down a few seconds later and she looked really pretty with her purple shirt greatly matching her hair which she had pulled back in a half up- half down hairdo.

"Let's go!"

Kyla opened the door and walked alongside her friends,

staring around her. She was in awe at the school. There were so many things for them to do not just in their customised rooms but also around the entire building. They even had a small petting zoo where they kept a baby of every creature to research in their class. As they were heading to the library Mackenzie, Ingrid and Daniel were in a very heated conversation over Changeball teams.

"You guys are joking right? There's no way that the rhinos are better than the falcons, no way at all. You guys are in fourth..." Mackenzie was arguing while Ingrid and Daniel shook their heads furiously.

"And you're now twelfth after your recent loss, what's your point? We are also in the semis of the intercontinental champions cup and we won the Changeball cup last year. While you guys have been on the decline since 2004, I mean you haven't even won a league in the last 20 years, while we won it only 3 seasons ago" Ingrid was saying angrily.

"Yeah, Mackenzie there is absolutely no way you are right on this one." Daniel argued. Mackenzie spun towards him, her eyes glinting dangerously.

"Oh yeah Daniel, suck up to Ingrid we all know..." she started before Kalen luckily cut in and interrupted her.

"Guys, guys." He held up his hands in calming gestures.

"Let's not fight about this when we all know that the eagles are in fact the best." He said it trying to calm the situation but at this, everyone began laughing and laughing at Kalen for suggesting that the eagles were a good team. It took Kyla and Kalen ten whole minutes to help the others subside their laughter. They had just passed the room with the animal samples when they heard some muttering near the library. They turned the corner and watched silently as Ms Smith was whispering with the librarian, Ms Newta.

"I'm telling you I can't find the book. I swear I had it at the start of the year but now it's gone. It makes no sense. I..." Newta was saying. However, it was at this point that Kyla zoned out for a minute as a large shadow had just passed overhead. She squinted suspiciously at it, but it surprisingly turned out to be just a fly. She refocused and heard-

"...Gone? It must have been misplaced when we were expanding the library, that's all. I'll order a new copy and we can put it back. How does that sound?" Ms Smith was saying. The librarian nodded and shuffled away. The 5 students watched silently when Ingrid started continuously tapping on Kyla's shoulder. She turned and saw that she was holding her nose and trying hard not to sneeze. Kyla only had time to whisper a warning before Ingrid let out 3 incredibly loud sneezes which echoed through the room. Ms Smith turned and smiled.

"Ok guys I know you're there. You can come out now."

Kyla motioned for the others to follow her, and she stepped into the library gaping at its enormity. Thousands of shelves stood surrounding her, filled from floor to ceiling with multicoloured books, all in alphabetical order of course. She loved it! Back home, Kyla's own room felt like a library, containing millions of different books. Kyla giggled excitedly. She would definitely be spending a lot of time in the library.

Daniel, on the other hand, stood behind her muttering "why so many books?" He kept grumbling as Kalen gaped and stared and stared and stared some more, completely in awe, even though he had likely already visited the library.

"You like it?" Gwenda said. Or maybe Kyla should call her Ms Smith now? It was all a bit confusing, but she chose to be formal and call her by her school's name.

"Yes." Kyla breathed.

Ms Smith smiled. "How was your first day?" Everyone echoed that it was good, and Ms Smith's smile widened. "I see you're all Optimistic Octopuses."

Kyla cringed and she could see all her friends flinch too.

"I take it you don't like the name?" Ms Smith laughed as

they all shook their heads ferociously. "No one does. I hate it too."

"Why don't you change it then?" Mackenzie demanded.

"It's Decker's own journey." She shrugged. "He needs to realise his ideas aren't the best."

"That's putting it mildly." Mackenzie muttered under her breath earning herself a harsh elbow to the ribs by Ingrid, who had clearly heard her. As had everyone else who were all now staring in her direction.

"Anyway." Gwenda said. "I see you have joined the gang, Ingrid."

"The gang?" Kyla, Daniel, Mackenzie, Kalen and Ingrid all shouted aghast.

"Seriously mom?" Kalen asked as Mackenzie groaned. It was at this moment that she died of cringe; or pretended to anyway. She clutched her heart and doubled over, gasping for breath.

Kyla rolled her eyes.

"Yes, I have joined the gang." Ingrid said, emphasising the word to show her own dislike.

"Ok I get it. It wasn't my best 'young people talk'." Ms Smith tucked one of her hairs behind her ear. "I guess you guys have some exploring to do, so have fun. I, on the other hand, have principal business." She yawned dramatically. "I hope you'll all come over to our house for Christmas."

"Isn't that like in 4 whole months' time?" Daniel asked.

"Yes, but I just wanted to assure you that you are all invited." She looked at Ingrid, who mumbled about likely not being able to but saying that she would ask her parents as soon as she got back to her house. With a one-armed hug from Kalen, Ms Smith departed, and the children were left in the dead silent library, all alone.

After several minutes of silently looking around, Daniel finally snapped saying "I'm out!" and everyone reluctantly followed him as he crossed the library and exited, closing the door harder than necessary. Kyla definitely heard a "SHHH!" from the librarian and decided to race forward and drag the others along with her. They were just passing the mythical creature's classroom when Kyla swore she saw a flicker of movement to the left and whispered voices. When she turned, however, she saw nothing and figured that it had been part of her imagination until Kalen came up beside her.

"Did you hear voices?" He whispered.

"I thought I was imagining them." Kyla replied just as quietly, she looked at where she had heard the sound coming from but still only saw a barely light corridor.

"It must be nothing." Kalen said but his voice was still soft, and his eyes scanned the corridor too.

"THAT'S NOT TRUE!" Someone shouted from the dark corridor and the voice sounded familiar somehow and so Kyla grabbed Kalen by the arm and went towards it. Mackenzie, Daniel and Ingrid followed and they found Delvin and Zilef in a very intense conversation.

Both boys stood facing each other, dark blue shirts on them, with a white ox on the back. Zilef looked on the verge of laughter, whilst Delvin looked downright furious.

"What's wrong?" Mackenzie asked and both boys spun, their eyes widening at the visitors. Zilef smiled at them, turning to Kyla as he spoke.

"I found Delvin walking around in the shadows acting all mysterious and holding a book." He laughed and held up a book, which had a familiar logo, probably because there was the same sign on every wall in Mackenzie's room. "Can you believe he's a Falcon's fan? They are sooooo bad!"

Zilef cracked up, whilst both Mackenzie and Delvin fumed, screaming "THAT'S NOT TRUE!". Daniel and Kalen also looked on the verge of laughter and Kyla didn't know whether to join them or be defensive like the others. She felt torn. She didn't know whether to support the eagles or the falcons. No way was she a fan of the Rhinos.

"I wasn't even acting mysterious!" Delvin protested.

"Uh. Hey, I'm not judging you. If I was a Falcon fan I would be embarrassed too. But you totally were." Zilef shot back. "You were walking around on your tippy toes dude!"

Delvin stared at his feet for a long second then his head snapped back up. "I was not!"

"Were too!" Zilef snapped.

"If I had wanted to sneak around, I would have changed into something small and quiet like a ladybug or a centipede." Delvin replied angrily.

He made a fair point.

"Moving on..." Kalen interrupted before things got out of hand. "What have you been doing Zilef?"

"Oh, you know. Hanging out with my new peeps. Trying to get some house spirit. Catching up with work..."

"We don't have work." Mackenzie interrupted but got completely ignored.

"Decorating my hut because my roommate is a complete moron, who prefers it to be boring." Delvin punched him in the gut, but he simply smiled. "Joking. Though you must see his room. It's all black and BORING!"

"What's yours like?" Kyla asked him.

"I can send you a pic if you want."

"I want to see too!" Daniel chimed in.

"Coming right up!" He said dramatically, then decided to add "As soon as I get to my house that is."

An alarm sounded and Mackenzie glanced at her wrist band. "Looks like it's time for dinner." She spoke. "Beat you there!"

Daniel scoffed. "You wish."

***

By the time they had finished stuffing their faces with the night's meal, which turned out to be pizza, Kyla was officially beat. She slowly raised from the table and after waving goodbye to her friends made her way back to her home with Mackenzie following her and talking to her the ENTIRE time with Kyla giving one syllable responses and occasionally a nod and a shrug. She was very grateful when they reached their rooms, and she was able to politely excuse herself. Knackered, she flopped down onto her bed and drifted off to sleep. But as she slept a nagging thought kept bothering her. Something was not right.

But...

What?

# CHAPTER 9

# **DANIEL**

"Today is going to be a good day." Daniel told Kalen as they made their way across the cafeteria and towards the breakfast line, which was growing significantly even though it was only 7:20 and breakfast started at 8:00.

Both Daniel and Kalen had slipped on their new 'Optimistic Octopus' house shirt at Rheas' command and now Daniel could see that both, Mackenzie and Kyla, had done the same. They looked like twins as the boys neared them in the breakfast line- they both wore their purple shirts and their hair tied back into two perfect braids. Kyla, however, wore a purple chequered skirt, whilst Mackenzie wore torn jeans.

"Good morning." He said formally.

Kyla hugged him then stepped back, pressing her

wristband under his eyes. "Zilef sent me a photo of his room."

She scrolled down a long conversation and showed Daniel a picture of a truly jam-packed room, with billions of posters of Changeball teams, though Daniel only recognised the logo of his own preferred squad- the rhinos. Splattered on the bed were multiple stacks of multicoloured comic books but Daniel barely saw them as Kyla zoomed into the far side of the picture which was populated with little holographic 3D creatures.

"He collects holograms too." She said excitedly. "He said he might be willing to trade double ups."

Daniel smiled, glad his sister had made another friend.

Kalen tapped him on the shoulder. "You were saying…? Today is going to be a good day?"

"Why's that?" Mackenzie asked, eyeing Daniel, who rolled his eyes at them for not spotting the obvious.

"We don't have Mr Smithy. Duh."

"Why do you hate him so much?" Kyla asked him. She stepped several places forward as the cue moved along. Only a few students stood between the four friends and their breakfast.

"I have a feeling I'm not going to enjoy his class." Daniel

grumbled. "I mean he rides a bright red scooter, for crying out loud!" He thrust his finger outwards, pointing towards the red shape zooming past huddles of students, shouting furiously to "MOVE OUT OF THE WAY LOSERS!"

Mackenzie shrugged. "I like him."

"You do?" Daniel, Kyla and Kalen all asked her, eyes widening with surprise.

"Why?" Kalen asked Mackenzie.

"He literally kicked you in the gut." Kyla reminded her but she simply shrugged again.

"I respect that." Mackenzie told them, grabbing a lunch tray and dumping several pancakes. She took the chocolate syrup from Kyla's hands (without asking) and sprayed the delicious liquid on the pancakes until they were fully submerged.

Daniel couldn't quite resist gaging. "Ugh. Why so much syrup?"

"Says the guy who has just picked icing-sugar-with-pancakes instead of pancakes-with-icing-sugar." Mackenzie shot back. She pointed at where his pancakes were covered with the delicate white sugar.

"Let's just agree you both have weird choices." Kyla said.

"Yeah. Could you two be any less healthy?" Kalen agreed.

His tray was stacked with fruits and he had copied Kyla's choice of poached eggs and a vanilla milkshake.

"Yeah Daniel. Grab a piece of fruit." Kyla ordered and Daniel sighed. He studied each fruit, picking an orange. He chose a very small orange on purpose, refusing to follow Kyla's instructions fully, and placed it on a section in his tray as well as a glass of hot chocolate.

They went over and sat at a wide table, which turned out to be the right choice as more people joined them. Ingrid plopped down in front of Daniel as Mackenzie huffed; Zilef sat opposite to Kalen and Delvin sat beside him. Gabbi, Lucus (a boy with ginger hair and brown streaks) and Livia (Kalen's partner in the magical creature's project, who had blond hair and pink streaks as well as sparkling blue eyes) joined in a few minutes later and the table was soon packed with people, who were laughing and chatting. Zilef joked about Mr Smithy's scooter, whilst Daniel frowned at the thought of the mentally deranged teacher racing behind him, chasing him for eternity.

His horrifying train of thoughts came to a sudden stop as a quiet voice asked "Can I join you?" behind him.

Daniel turned, meeting Vasquez, who looked extremely shy and kept looking at the ground. He was incredibly tall and his brown eyes were quite large. His spiky black and red hair stood up from his head and complimented his dark skin tone.

"Of course." Daniel pointed to the seat next to him but Vasquez shook his head and leaned in close to him.

"Can I talk to you for a second?"

"Ok." Daniel replied, looking at his sister who shot him a nowhere near subtle tell-me-everything-later-look which was noticed by everyone, Daniel was sure that even Mr Smithy had seen it. He rolled his eyes then tilted his chin towards the farthest corner in the canteen, motioning for Vasquez to follow. Once they were in the quiet space, away from everyone, Daniel asked Vasquez what was wrong.

"I actually don't know why I'm telling you this." Vasquez muttered. "I don't know why I figured telling you was a good idea."

"Maybe tell me what it is and then we decide if it was a good idea or a bad one?" Daniel said.

"Ok." Vasquez paused long enough for Daniel to raise his eyebrows and do continuous actions with his hands. A few minutes passed and Daniel was about to leave and go back to the lovely, peaceful breakfast, when Vasquez finally spoke.

"I guess… umm. It's about our magical creature's project. My creature was tampered with." he mumbled and Daniel felt his eyes widen.

"How so?"

"Remember how Ms Orgi lectured us on the aggressiveness level? And how she ordered us to keep it at a very low level?" Vasquez let that sink in. "Well, it's been changed. To the highest level."

Daniel gasped. "For your creature?"

"For all the ones I've checked."

"Maybe it was by accident?"

"All of them? Not likely." His brown eyes stared into Daniel's, leaving no trace of doubt.

Daniel didn't know what to do with that information. He definitely didn't like it but he thanked Vasquez and led him back to their table to eat. When he sat he noticed his sister trying to catch his attention but he ignored her, mentally replaying what Vasquez had told him.

How odd. He thought. First the raptor DNA. Now their own creations.

He smiled. He was obviously overreacting. It was probable that Ms Orgi had just changed her mind.

Right?

***

"Of course not!" Ms Orgi snapped during first class.

Daniel backed up a step as she raced past him, towards the test tubes. She opened a computer screen and began typing furiously until she found his groups' DNA samples. She showed it to Daniel.

The aggressive levels weren't any higher than normal and Daniel couldn't see anything wrong with them though the glare he was receiving from Ms Orgi really made him wish she had found something wrong. However, when he explained what had happened Ms Orgi promised to look into it and told him to sit back down next to Ingrid. Dejected he sat down and listened half-heartedly to Ingrid injecting the DNA samples into their incubator.

"Hello?"

Daniel snapped back to the present to find a hand being waved in front of his face and Ingrid's teal eyes staring into his brown ones.

"Yes?" Daniel asked.

Ingrid's sigh carried through the whole class and Daniel was sure that everyone was now staring at them; or maybe it was only Mackenzie who glared as if Daniel had disturbed her peace and quiet.

"Ok." Ingrid whispered, leaning in. "What's wrong?"

Daniel flinched as he muttered the world's least convincing "I'm fine".

Ingrid leaned even closer. "I know this has something to do with what Vasquez told you at breakfast."

"No it doesn't!" Daniel lied. Or tried to but his squeak gave him away. He really needed to get better at lying.

"Fine, don't tell me!" Ingrid hissed, turning her back on him. It was an obvious attempt at luring Daniel to spill what was bothering him and it worked. Soon, Daniel felt himself sighing and mumbling everything he knew and every word he had spoken with Vasquez and Ms Orgi.

"Wow." Ingrid breathed once Daniel's 5-minute-long explanation had come to an end. She looked around and Daniel realised that no one was looking their way- which was a relief. Apart from Kyla, who was narrowing her eyes as if she suspected something. He rolled his eyes at her and continued working on the creature with Ingrid but she was too distracted to really concentrate. Daniel honestly didn't blame her, it was very, very strange. Or it was until he heard Malcom snickering behind him. He turned and saw him pointing at him laughing and saying stuff like 'prank' and 'aggressive'. Ingrid followed his gaze and narrowed her eyes at Malcom and his cronies.

"Well, I guess that explains why you were acting strange." she said, though she still sounded suspicious. In fact, she wouldn't take her eyes off Malcom for two whole minutes, and only stopped when Daniel told her it might look a little bit weird.

"So, should we continue with our creature?" Ingrid said loudly, pretending to adjust the DNA.

" I think we should call him Mr Furry face" she said looking at the DNA sequence lovingly. It was obviously a subject change from their previous conversation and she shot Daniel a look that said that the conversation clearly wasn't over.

"Uh no. We are not going to call him something ridiculous like that. He needs a respectable name, something that is actually inspiring and cool and awesome. A true hero." Daniel said.

"Let me guess. Something like Batman?"

"Huh. NO! That is, simply, a ridiculous name." Daniel scoffed, then rolled his eyes. "It should be called Daniel jr. Obviously."

"Yeah. No way." She said cringing, which left Daniel feeling slightly offended. "Wait, I got it! Let's call it Pyror."

"Not as good as Daniel jr but I'll accept it." He held out his hand and Ingrid shook it, laughing.

"I think it's ready to go. Let's ask Ms Orgi." Ingrid grabbed Daniel by the arm but he resisted, thinking about how Ms Orgi was really stressed because of him.

"How about you go and ask?" He said.

Ingrid must've seen something in his expression because she didn't argue. She just nodded and left towards the teacher desk. Daniel on the other hand started going around the room, stopping by each friend. Kalen was with Livia, who was extremely nice and started a conversation with Daniel, asking him how his creature was going, what it was like to work with Ingrid and whether or not he thought the creature would be hard to take care of. Daniel could tell Kalen and Livia worked really well together. Livia excused herself, winking her blue eyes and saying that her hair needed to get tied up.

Daniel left Kalen and moved to the other side of the class where he found Mackenzie and Gabbi working together.

"Hey." He said and Gabbi turned towards the sound of his voice, whilst Mackenzie barely looked up from where she sat, sketching.

"Finished your creature?" Mackenzie asked without even a glance at Daniel.

"Yep. How's yours going?" He directed the question at Mackenzie but Gabbi answered.

"We're done." She said. Her body towered over Daniel's very short one. "We need to go tell Ms Orgi."

"What's Mackenzie doing then?"

"Getting bored to death." Mackenzie muttered, scrunching up the paper and throwing it into the bin without even looking.

"Nice shot." Daniel praised and Mackenzie shrugged.

"Have you and Zilef finished yours?" She asked and Daniel opened his mouth to say that he had Ingrid as a partner when another voice answered.

"Yes." Daniel had never jumped quite so high in his life. He turned and found Kyla smirking at him. "Didn't you hear me?"

"How do you walk around so quietly with such big feet?" He asked, earning himself an elbow to the ribs.

"Foot insults aside." Kyla smiled. "We're shapeshifters."

"Yeah." Zilef said behind her and this time everyone jumped- except Mackenzie who seemed completely aware of where everyone was in the room. She didn't even flinch, though she did mutter a lot about unwanted visitors.

"DANIEL!" He whipped around and saw Ingrid racing

towards him with an egg.

"Ooh. Are we having omelette for lunch?" He reached towards the egg but Ingrid swatted his hand away.

"Daniel!" She shrieked and he had to continuously assure her that he was merely joking around. He would never eat the beautiful creation that lay inside.

"Come to PAPA Dan." He took the white and black egg and rocked it around like a baby as everyone asked "PAPA Dan?"

Mackenzie rolled her eyes. "Seriously?"

Before Daniel could reply, Gabbi grabbed Mackenzie's arm and yanked her towards the teacher's desk, giggling at the thought of getting their own egg. Kyla, on the other hand, examined Daniel and Ingrid's egg, claiming that hers and Zilef's was better. Daniel had to agree that it was gorgeous as the teal colour sparkled and glinted in the light, giving off a breathtaking effect, which made it look magical. But there was no way that egg was better than his own.

The twins spent at least ten minutes arguing about which was the better egg, until Ms Orgi finally declared the end of class, stating that the next part of the project was to take it in turns looking after the creatures. Ingrid volunteered to look after Pyror first but Daniel argued.

She leaned in close to whisper in his ear. "I'll drop him off at your house after lunch when you update me on everything."

Just as Daniel was heading towards the door she added something else.

"Bring Mackenzie and Kalen." She told him. "Definitely bring Kyla. Her glare looks deadly."

# CHAPTER 10

## KYLA

Kyla tapped her foot furiously on the floor of her brother's room, refusing to give an end to her powerful glare. Up until right then, she hadn't known anything about Vasquez's conversation or about the strangeness surrounding the creatures. She hadn't even paid much attention to the missing raptor DNA samples, which was a mistake on her part. She should've been more vigilant.

But that wasn't the reason as to why she was fuming. First, she found out her brother was ignoring her and then she realised that he had confided in somebody else before telling his own twin sister. Talk about twin betrayal.

A tiny smile did slip onto her lips when she saw Daniel's guilty expression but it soon vanished as she growled angrily and turned away.

"I know you're mad." Daniel said, holding his hands up like he would in an ambush. "And you have every right to be. I'm sorry."

"For what?" Kyla snapped. "For ignoring me? For telling Ingrid everything before telling me? For only including me in this conversation when Ingrid told you to?"

Her brother flinched with each question and Kyla wanted to continue listing things but his pitiful eyes stopped her. Why were his eyes so cute and puppy-like? She thought angrily.

"Look, I told you now." He said.

"Because Ingrid told you to."

"I was going to tell you." He promised and his eyes pleaded for her to believe him.

A loud cough rang out and the door to the room swung forward as well as multiple bodies which fell on top of each other. Mackenzie on the other hand, sauntered over them and towards Kyla.

"We were eavesdropping." She admitted. "And don't you dare let him down easily."

Daniel sighed, dragging a hand down his face, whilst Ingrid got up from where she had fallen on top of Kalen and Zilef.

"I forced him to tell me." She said, defending Daniel and Kyla directed her glare at her instead but her brother stood up and approached her.

"Okay. How about you dare me to do anything you want?"

An evil smile formed on Kyla's lips as well as Mackenzie's. "I'm listening." They said simultaneously.

"Not you." He said pointing at Mackenzie, who gave him a dirty look and walked over to his bed. "And Kyla, you can only give me one dare. Only. One."

Kyla scratched her chin, thinking of all the possibilities. Then she realised that she could leave her brother sweating and in suspense. "I'll think about it."

Daniel narrowed his eyes. He clearly knew what she was up to but he didn't argue and flopped back onto the bed next to Mackenzie.

"Ok. Everyone's been caught up. So the question is what are we going to do now?" He asked.

"We need to investigate!" Mackenzie shouted, launching herself off the bed, pulling out a magnifying glass from thin air and examining around the room. She went up to Ingrid and started looking at her through the magnifying glass, pulling her hair and arms close so she could scrutinise her.

"Not here, we don't." Zilef said, saving Ingrid from further inspecting as he dragged Mackenzie away from her. "And also, we don't even know what to investigate, much less whether we should."

"What do you mean?" Kyla asked him.

"Well, we only have Vasquez's word about the tampering. Daniel said Ms Orgi checked and everything was normal so how do we know something has changed?" He looked guiltily at Daniel. "I'm not saying I don't trust Vasquez. It's just he didn't have any proof."

"That's what I thought too." Ingrid added. "And also, no offence, but why tell Daniel and not anyone else? Vasquez didn't even tell the teachers."

"That's what I thought too." Mackenzie admitted, though she looked disgusted at agreeing with Ingrid. "I mean if he should've told any of us he should've told me!"

"And why is that?" Kyla groaned, smacking her head.

"Because Detective Mac's on a roll." Mackenzie puffed out her chest. "I've solved sixteen mysteries this past month."

"Almost all of them were a search for her dad's socks." Kalen whispered, dodging Mackenzie's brutal kick, which would've left him collapsed on the floor. Kyla laughed.

"We need to see if what Vasquez said is true." Daniel said, standing up but Kyla stopped him before he could leave.

"And how do you suppose we do that?" Kyla asked. "Ms Orgi already checked."

"But maybe she checked it in a different way to Vasquez." Ingrid mumbled, her eyes widening as everyone turned their attention to her. She seemed at a loss of words as if she had mumbled the words mostly to herself, not wanting anyone to hear them.

"That's genius!" Kalen shouted and Ingrid blushed as Mackenzie grumbled under her breath.

"We need to find Vasquez." Daniel concluded, heading for the door but Kyla stopped him again.

"We should go to the library."

"Now is not the time to get nerdy." Daniel protested and Kyla rolled her eyes.

"We need to know what increasing aggressiveness does to the creatures." She argued. It was a perfectly logical plan and she could see Zilef and Ingrid nodding but her brother didn't seem convinced so she thought of a compromise.

"Ok." Kyla said. "Take Mackenzie and Kalen with you to see Vasquez and the rest of us will go to the library."

"Sounds good." Ingrid and Mackenzie said simultaneously. Mackenzie "humphed" and grabbed both Kalen and Daniel by the arms, leading them out of the room.

"Ok." Kyla grinned, excited by the thought of adventure. "Let's go!"

***

The only sound that echoed in the silent studying atmosphere was the click of their shoes against the blue obsidian floor of the library. Kyla breathed in every peaceful second, deciding that this was definitely one of her favourite places in the whole facility. The entire place sparkled with crystal walls and different forms of chairs littered the area. There were hammocks, bean bag chairs, couches; it was a paradise. There were even more shelves than there were the last time Kyla had been there and the information desk stood on a raised platform made of bright pink obsidian. Ms Newta- the librarian- stood there, with her crystal glasses perched on the tip of her nose and her eyes glancing over at Kyla and her friends. She was obviously annoyed by the little noise they were making and she pointed at the quiet sign next to her desk.

"Sorry." Kyla said as they approached the desk. "We were wondering if you could please help us?"

Kyla's manners threw Ms Newta back a step and left her smiling warmly. "Of course!"

"It's for a project on magical creatures." Ingrid started.

Before they had entered, Zilef had proposed a plan and script, stating that they would likely need a reason for their thirst for knowledge and Kyla had instantly agreed. They had settled on needing the information for a magical creature project which wasn't far from the truth and therefore didn't mean they were lying if they got caught. Kyla clutched the script tightly in her hand as her nerves increased but Ingrid seemed confident.

"We were wondering if there is a book with the details we need to create a creature?" Ingrid said.

"There are many." Ms Newta said flatly. "You need to be more specific."

Ingrid looked at Kyla, who nodded, indicating that she should continue. "We need to know about adjusting DNA, modifying genes, aggressiveness levels…"

Ms Newta looked at them apologetically. "Oh dear, I'm afraid someone took it yesterday!"

All three of them turned towards each other and Kyla felt her jaw drop.

"Who took it?" Kyla asked urgently.

"It was…"

"Yes?" Zilef and Ingrid pressed, when Ms Newta scratched her head. Kyla already knew the answer and her heart sank at the realisation.

"You don't know, do you?" Kyla asked and the librarian shook her head.

"How is that possible?" Zilef cried. "Didn't you see their face?"

"I didn't." Ms Newta said plainly. "If that is all then you can leave. There are students waiting behind you."

With that, Kyla, Ingrid and Zilef shuffled out, rather reluctantly as they all wanted to know more. Kyla's mind spun in a million different directions as thousands of thoughts circled around in her brain as well as one question.

Who?

She was so caught up in that question that she didn't realise where she was going until she barged into something with a loud THUMP!

"OW!" A high-pitched shriek sounded from above Kyla, who had fallen and ended up covered in thick books. She looked up at the girl who had shrieked. She wasn't exactly tall but she wasn't necessarily short either and her confident posture was intimidating enough. Her almost white hair was tied into a bun with several grey strands sticking out and her intense sea green eyes glared at Kyla.

"Sorry." Kyla mumbled. She grabbed the books around her and stood up to give them to the girl.

"You better be." The girl sneered, snatching the books from Kyla's hands. "You're that girl aren't you?"

"Um…"

"Malcom was right. You are unbearable!" The girl said, with a revolted look and rolling her eyes.

Kyla felt a surge of anger and her insides boiled with uncontrollable fury. "You don't even know me!"

"I know enough." The girl turned to stalk away but stopped as she noticed Ingrid standing beside Kyla. "Ugh. Don't get me started on Ms Royalty. Ugh. Just ugh."

Kyla hooked her arm through Ingrids' before she could launch herself on the rude girl and Zilef placed a hand on both of their shoulders, leading them out. Before they passed the girl, however, Kyla felt something slide below her feet and the next second she was on the floor. The girl had tripped her!

"She's not worth it." Zilef said before Kyla could strike her fist into the girl. She settled on glowering instead and he reached out a hand to help her up.

"Who is she?" Kyla asked disgustedly.

"Zila." Ingrid spat out. "Worst girl you'll ever meet."

Somehow Kyla doubted it and she knew this wouldn't be the last time she would have to deal with the girl's snotty attitude. She stared back towards the library desk but Zila had vanished, leaving only the trail of dropped books behind. Ingrid's wristwatch buzzed on and she picked up the call.

"Kalen said they talked to Vasquez and apparently there's a creature check section in the magical creature DNA storehouse." She said, once she had finished.

"That's great!" Zilef said. He started to make his way to the hallway before Ingrid stopped him.

"It's on constant surveillance." Ingrid said, bursting his bubble. "No way of getting in without Ms Orgi realising. Not in broad daylight at least."

"At night then." Kyla suggested. "We'll scout the area tonight."

Ingrid looked up shyly. "Oh… um, here's the thing. Tonight are the Changeball try-outs, and I really wanted to see it live. Who knows how long they'll last."

Kyla smacked her forehead. "Right. I forgot. Daniel, Mackenzie, Kalen and I need to go to the try-outs too. I guess that's off then."

"Not necessarily. I can go." Zilef suggested. Kyla and Ingrid spun around to face him.

"Don't you want to try out?" Ingrid asked.

"Nah I don't really mind and besides I'm an Ox not an

Octopus."

Now Kyla felt guilty. After all, it had been her idea. "Are you sure you want to go? And by yourself too?"

"Yeah. It'll be extra stealthy." He assured her and his confident smirk settled the argument.

***

"Get up!" Decker shrieked.

Kyla leaned down to help Kalen up, who unfortunately, seemed to be the person Decker's anger was directed towards. His eyes were narrowed at the poor, sweaty boy and he kept shouting at every action Kalen did wrong.

Decker was the older boy who had some of the worst ideas ever. For example: naming the house "Optimistic Octopuses." His black, shortly cropped hair was mixed with brown streaks the same colour as his eyes and his slightly smeared glasses were propped up on his nose. He stormed over to Kalen and pulled him up roughly.

"You're pathetic!" He shouted. Ingrid, who was trying to learn about Changeball coaching, glared at him.

"No he's not!" She said,

Ms Orgi came up behind her. "Decker." She said angrily.

"You may be the house captain this year but you are not the coach and I think Kalen is doing an amazing job."

Decker scoffed.

Ms Orgi rounded on him and he stepped away from her in fright. "Don't you dare! Don't you DARE doubt my coaching opinions and discredit Mr Smith!"

Decker turned and left, probably on his way to insult other first years who were trying out for the Changeball team. Ms Orgi huffed and stormed after him.

Kyla turned to Kalen encouragingly. "You're doing great!"

Kalen turned red. "You and Mackenzie got past me easily."

"That's because we're amazing!" Kalen and Ingrid jumped but Kyla just turned towards Mackenzie, far too used to the way that she just appeared out of thin air all of a sudden. Kyla wasn't prepared for Daniel though, and she almost jumped out of her skin at the sudden sight of him.

Daniel smirked. "I don't know about that." He flashed a confident smile. "I saved plenty of shots."

"Kyla scored more." Kalen replied with a smug smile.

"She wouldn't have if you had defended." Daniel snapped at him.

"She wouldn't have if you had saved her shots." he

snapped back.

Ingrid stepped between them. "Wow. Calm your horses, you two!"

One thing Kyla had learnt: shapeshifters tended to use animal sayings a lot. For example Zilef kept texting her constantly about Mr Smithy being an old bat (someone annoying or unpleasant, which Mr Smithy definitely was.) It had been pretty embarrassing when she had replied to Zilef's text, explaining that she didn't know what he was saying and so he sent her 'normal' sayings everyday now. He called it the 'cool talk of the day'.

"Seriously." Kyla said. "I was just too good for both of you." She high fived Mackenzie who grinned at Daniel's shocked expression. Out of all of them Mackenzie was probably the most likely to make it on the team as she had easily dodged past defenders and scored multiple goals against the other goalies. Daniel had also made some pretty impressive saves, catching a ball in mid-air with a giant leap. Kyla felt pretty confident about all their chances and couldn't help smiling confidently. The smile only lasted a few seconds as Decker's annoying voice screamed more orders.

Mackenzie glared in his direction. "How many days until the end of the year?"

"Too many to count." Daniel said and they both groaned.

"Cheer up guys." Ingrid said cheerfully. "One more minute and then off to bed!"

Mackenzie gasped, appalled. "To bed?" She asked. "It's only midnight! Think of all the pranks we could pull?"

Daniel smirked. "I was thinking we could go to…"

"No!" Kyla interrupted, not wanting to hear any of her brother's devious little plans. "You need to rest for school tomorrow."

"I can sleep in Ms Hinkle's class." He argued. "Or Mr Butland's. They always make the most boring lectures."

"Only because you laugh at their names." Kalen reminded him. The whistle had blown, declaring the end of the try-outs. The five friends told Ms Orgi good night and left towards their dorms.

"The names are hilarious!" Mackenzie snorted. "Hinkle tinkles. Butt-land."

"They're kind of rude." Ingrid observed, which only seemed to make Mackenzie love them more.

"It's not my fault they have such teasable names." Daniel protested and Kyla begrudgingly agreed that he had a point. She tried to hide it and lowered her head to hide her smile. They walked over the patches of grass, discussing the various ridiculous names as they went, though Kalen kept noticeably quiet and walked behind everyone else. Kyla fell into step with him but stayed silent, not wanting to press him. It was only after Ingrid left to her hut that Kalen spoke.

"What are you doing?" He asked.

"Walking beside you." She said matter of factly but Kalen shook his head.

"Why?"

"You were falling behind." She said but seeing Kalen's frown she couldn't help asking what was wrong.

"Nothing." He said. Kyla wasn't convinced.

"I know somethings wrong." She said, looking him in the eye but he turned away and kept walking. He refused to talk so she was forced to use plan B. "I know somethings wrong, so you can either tell me or I can guess. And I have many guesses. Embarrassing ones."

Kalen shrugged but Kyla's plan had clearly worked as he mumbled something.

"What?" She asked.

He sighed. "I'm afraid I won't make the team."

"What? I still can't hear you." she said in a singsong voice.

"I said I'm afraid I won't make the team." He repeated but Kyla shook her head, laughing.

"I heard you the first time. Why won't you make the team?"

He stopped and crossed his arms in front of him. "You're kidding right? I was so bad!"

"WHAT?" Kalen flinched at her shout but she couldn't help it. "You were by far the best defender there! You stopped me from scoring like ten times!"

"You still scored and you heard Decker!" He slouched. "I'm pathetic."

His ice blue eyes looked so sad that Kyla felt herself reach forward and place a comforting hand on his back. She waited until he looked up at her. "You'll make the team. You'll see."

Her words seemed to get to him and he sighed. "Thanks. I'll see you tomorrow." With that, he walked over to his hut, stepping between Mackenzie and Daniel, who were (to no one's surprise) arguing about their Changeball teams. Their heated argument came to a sudden halt, however, as they noticed Kalen move between them.

Mackenzie frowned. "What's wrong with him?"

"He doesn't think he'll make the team." Kyla told her and instead of giving some words of encouragement, Mackenzie turned and raced into her own house.

"I'll talk to him." Daniel said, wishing his sister a

goodnight. He waved from the front porch then opened the door and slipped inside.

After such an exhausting day, Kyla barely had the energy to take a shower but she somehow managed it and within half an hour, she had changed into her pyjamas and was yanking her bed covers over herself. She shouted goodnight to Mackenzie and surprisingly received a response as her friend wished her a restful night. Every bone in Kyla's body ached and as soon as her head rested on the soft pillow her eyes closed and she fell into a slumber.

Unfortunately, it wasn't a peaceful one.

Darkness invaded her mind as she replayed all the horrid flashbacks from the past days. The house exploding. Her brother missing. Her mom getting taken. But somewhere in between the past lay something else. Something sinister. Something real. Something that made her sweat, itch, turn, flinch, twist...scream.

"MOM!"

Her mom's face appeared in her mind, twisted in agony, surrounded by darkness. She screamed and thrashed consistently but to no avail; she was stuck. Her wrists were bound so tightly that an ugly red rash had started to form and Kyla could see the start of an infection. Suddenly, her mom's head snapped up.

"Kyla?" She whispered and she stared directly at her daughter as if she knew she was watching her.

A sinister laugh echoed around the blackness. "Hallucinating about your children again?" A snide voice sneered. It sounded familiar in some way and left Kyla's hair on end. She tried to turn around but for some reason she couldn't. She had no control over this nightmare.

All she could do was watch.

The ominous voice continued. "You didn't tell us where they were but don't worry. We happen to have eyes on them. Someone powerful has things covered in that school of theirs."

Her mom's eyes widened in fear and she quickly looked away from Kyla. "I don't know what you're talking about."

"Don't lie!" The voice snapped. "We've found them. We've found the twins."

"And soon we'll have them in our grasp!"

# CHAPTER 11

# **DANIEL**

"Ok, let me get this straight." Daniel spoke, passing a hand through his hair and trying to make it look good.

He snorted. Who was he kidding? His hair always looked awesome. Even at 5 am in the morning.

"Our mom is captured by a strange voice, which feels vaguely familiar to you and now that voice supposedly has its eyes on us and is coming to get us?" He stopped pacing on the newly changed, clear glass floor of his sister's room. He could see tiny fish swimming around underneath and wondered how she had managed to get such a cool floor. Her whole room looked pretty cool actually. She had a rock-climbing wall, a slide, a zipline, a roller skate rink and even a small pool.

The only thing missing was a TV, but then again, Kyla had

never truly been one to love watching films or play video games.

Kyla nodded at her brother. "There's always the possibility that it was just a dream." She shrugged.

"We all know it wasn't a dream." Kalen said from where he sat next to Daniel on the bean bag chairs. "I mean, it wasn't a normal dream."

"I know." She mumbled, staring down at her hands. "I mean, it was as if someone else was controlling my dream. I couldn't change it."

"I've had dreams like that too." Daniel admitted. All of them had been about a dark ominous voice speaking gibberish into the darkness but what if that hadn't been a dream. What if...

"What if it wasn't a dream? What if you saw what was happening then and there?" He asked his sister. Her brows scrunched together and she shivered.

"You guys are focusing on the wrong thing." Mackenzie said. She raced towards them so casually that Daniel didn't even realise that she was wearing skates until he looked down. "You are being targeted!"

"Yeah, I think we should let my mom know and get you security." Kalen reasoned but Mackenzie frowned at him and shook her head.

"Why?" She asked confused, then looked back at the twins, an excited gleam in her eyes. "You're being targeted! You should be training, fighting, punching people in the gut, spinning around, transforming into vicious beasts…"

"We get it." Kalen interrupted earning a glare from Mackenzie. "You wish you were targeted. Geez."

Mackenzie rolled her eyes. "That's not what I'm saying. I just want to ask: What are you going to do about it?"

She stomped her foot for emphasis, but seemed to forget that she was wearing skates and so she tumbled forward. Luckily, having her incredible reflexes she managed to somehow stop her momentum and righten herself up. Unfortunately, she didn't see where she was going, as she was too busy grinning, and so ended up smacking into the rock-climbing wall.

Everyone burst out laughing at her look of surprise. Mackenzie glared at them all.

Kyla recovered first and looked at her brother, a fiery intensity in her eyes. "We need to rescue mom."

"But how?" Daniel whined. He didn't want to sound so depressed but he couldn't help it. All this time he had been hoping to find their mother but now with the weird dream and the sinister voice he didn't feel like it would be possible.

"I don't know the whole plan yet." She admitted. "But I do know step one: find the mole."

"Sorry but shouldn't that be like step seven?" Kalen pointed out. "I mean we need a plan to find the mole don't we? Is there even proof that there's a mole?"

Daniel saw his sister think about that for a second. "If my dream wasn't a dream then there definitely is a mole. But you're right. We need a plan. But you get what I mean. Find the mole. Find our mom."

"It's not going to be that easy. It's just us." Daniel reminded her.

"Excuse me!" Mackenzie shouted. "You have me! The best detective in the whole world?"

Kalen coughed something that sounded very much like "that's debatable" but Mackenzie ignored him as she pulled off her skates. "First off, has anyone been in contact with Zilef?"

Daniel saw Kyla smack her forehead and he felt like doing the same. "We forgot completely."

Mackenzie smirked. "Good thing I didn't." She strolled over to put the skates away but then changed her mind. "Can I keep these?"

"Uh. Sure?" Kyla said, confused. She looked at Daniel with a face that seemed to ask is she for real? Then she turned back to Mackenzie. "You were saying?"

"Right. So I talked to Zilef since no one else seemed to have done so and he told me that he explored the DNA storehouse and someone definitely tampered with the creatures. The aggressive levels were off the charts."

"Did he find out who?" Daniel whispered.

"You know you don't have to whisper right?" Mackenzie scoffed. "Anyway. He didn't find out who. Whoever it was didn't leave any evidence behind but he said that the whole time he was there it felt as if someone was watching him and his every move. Watching. Listening. Waiting."

Everyone shivered.

"He said he left quickly and didn't explore too much because it gave him the creeps. Coward." She muttered.

"Hey! He did all he could." Kyla argued. "He was alone because we were all at Changeball try-outs!"

"I should've gone with him." Kalen mumbled softly and Daniel turned towards him.

"I thought you weren't moody anymore."

"Ok STOP!" Mackenzie screamed. "I do NOT want to see a sad, depressed little boy."

"I'm not depressed." Kalen whispered in a way that definitely sounded whiny and depressed to Daniel.

"Sure." Mackenzie said, her tone dripping with sarcasm. "But Kyla might have a point. Ugh that was so hard to say! Wait, I need to clear my throat." She gasped for breath dramatically. "Ok my point is: eight eyes are better than one."

"You mean two." Daniel corrected.

"No, I mean one. Have you seen the guy's eyesight? Each eye counts as half."

Daniel remembered the horrible target practice the day before, in Life skills. Ms Hinkle had rambled on and on after Zilef had impaled Malcom for the fifth time in a row. She lectured them for hours but it was fine because Daniel was too busy constantly replaying his enemy's pained expression and shrill scream.

"Good point".

"So I say we scout the place again. Tonight. All of us." Mackenzie eyed everyone in turn until they all nodded.

"I'll tell Zilef and Ingrid." Kyla said, standing up.

"No!" Mackenzie cried a little too quickly. "Just us. Definitely not Ingrid. I mean, we don't want to bother her or Zilef."

This came as a little bit of a surprise to Daniel even though it shouldn't have. He was well aware of Mackenzie's great dislike towards Ingrid though he didn't really comprehend it.

Girls.

"I agree." Kalen said with a quick glance at Kyla. "Look, Zilef already checked so there's no point in him coming again."

"True." She checked her watch hurriedly. "We should meet after school. We're going to be late."

Daniel sucked in a breath and jumped suddenly. "Mr Smithy is going to kill us! He's going to kill me!"

"No he won't." Mackenzie laughed but everyone else was rushing around packing their bags, pulling on their shoes and grabbing any food they could find for a quick breakfast. They had no time to waste!

"He won't kill you because you're his favourite." Kalen said, then muttered "surprisingly." Mackenzie slapped him across the arm.

"Ow!"

***

"Ow!"

The room was buzzing with "Ow" within the first five

seconds of self-defence class. Why?

Mr Smithy.

But most importantly: Mr Smithy's bright red, pain inflicting scooter. It whizzed past students with the miniature old man sitting at the wheel, launching balloons at absolutely everyone.

Balloons, which turned out to not be filled with water. Instead they were filled with little leprechauns that clung to the students and bit them until they gave up their most valuable belongings.

Daniel could see Kalen already getting beat up by the small creatures whilst Kyla was busy kicking one in its little face and then apologising when the leprechaun stumbled backward clutching its tiny head. Eventually she realised that it was all a trick as the creature bared its teeth and raced towards her with claws dangerously outstretched. Mackenzie, on the other hand, hadn't even been attacked yet. She sat in the corner of the room, looking at her nails, not at all bothered by the racket of the class. Daniel was pretty sure he saw her fall asleep for a few minutes, in fact she was sleeping right then, her knees curled in under her, a pillow slipped under her head.

Daniel shook his head, shocked.

A pillow? Where did that come from?

He had no time to puzzle over it as the teacher had spotted him. An evil smile spread across Mr Smithy's lips and he stepped on the gas, accelerating. Daniel gasped and ran to the other end of the room, hearing the beeping of the scooter behind him getting closer. Balloons flew past him, leprechauns chased after him, Malcom sneered at him (and of course Daniel glared back at the boy). But he didn't stop running.

"Get back here! You little moron!" The teacher shrieked.

There was something about being chased by a grumpy ancient man that made Daniel's legs run faster than ever before and he bolted past everyone, not looking back. There was only one way to safety.

Mr Smithy's raised platform.

Daniel tore through the madness of the lesson and got to the throne-like chair in the middle of the class. He scanned everywhere for the remote to raise the platform but couldn't find it. Finally, he spotted it below the steps and lunged for it. He pressed a button.

Mr Smithy let out a shriek. "Stop! Don't press that!"

Daniel pressed it and turned around, laughing at what he saw. "Seriously? A poster of Darth Sidious? Wait, is that you? Photoshopped into it?"

The teacher's face burned tomato red. "That is my immature twin brother. Yes. That's a good lie. Totally believable. Yes. Yes. The moron will fall for it for sure. Yes. Yes. It's not as if he knows about my obsession with the dark side. Yes. Yes. A brother. Hmmm. A brother. Yes. Yes. hmmm…"

"You do notice we can hear you right?" Mackenzie called from the other side of the room in a sleepy voice.

"Sure you can. Sure you can. Sure you can…"

"AHEM!" Vasquez snapped Mr Smithy back to the present and the teacher glared at Daniel.

"Give me the remote! Give it! Give it! Give it back!"

That's it! Daniel thought as Mr Smithy stamped his feet on his scooter in frustration like a baby throwing a tantrum. This teacher's insane!

He rushed over to the platform and started pressing all the buttons, which turned out to be a grave mistake. The walls all around the class started opening up with sharp shards of glass jutting out dangerously near the other students. One of them grazed Kyla's shoulder and she recoiled in pain.

Mr Smithy suddenly gasped, his old face wrinkling even more than usual as he took in the chaos around him. He smiled. Then he started laughing. And laughing.

And laughing.

In fact, the old bat was laughing so much that he fainted right then and there, on top of his scooter, a bit of drool escaping his mouth and getting smeared around the controls. The entire class was dead silent. Then Vasquez cleared his throat with a loud "AHEM!". But the old man did not stir.

The students were about to celebrate when at that moment an alarm started ringing from his scooter. Mr Smithy snapped up and turned it off. He then went on to ignore the children and sped out of the class on his scooter screaming "SPRING ROLL SUNDAY!!" and pushing little kids and other teachers out of the way. He even shoved Ms Smith out of the way, though he was going so fast she probably didn't even notice it was him. The rest of the students stared at each other in confusion, shrugged and shuffled out of the classroom, the majority of them supporting bruises or broken bones or in most instances, both. Daniel sat next to Zilef in the cafeteria and was too exhausted to make any sort of conversation with anyone, merely shrugging and nodding to most of his friends' questions. When it was time to go to Practical Shapeshifting, Daniel was wrecked and he could see most of the class were too. In fact the only people who weren't hurt were Mackenzie and, surprisingly, Ingrid, which appeared to annoy Mackenzie even more than usual (which is really saying something).

When Monsieur Pris arrived he was in shock at the state of the class.

"What on Earth has happened here?" he asked in a thick French accent. Once again, Daniel couldn't help but find it weird as France was a country on Earth, not Ocelia. The entire class started mumbling about Mr Smithy which drew a look of absolute horror to his face.

"Ah yes the old Smitheroo. Wait, don't tell him I said that! We all know his hatred for nicknames." Monsieur Pris' face contorted in a painful expression as if he was reliving horrible memories. "I am so sorry for your pain. Especially you Mr Whixx. What has happened to you?"

"I appear to be the one who he hates the most, sir." Daniel muttered, eyeing his scars as he bandaged them up.

Monsieur Pris moved towards him and patted him on the shoulder. "You know, I wasn't his favourite student either."

Monsieur Pris didn't look too old but he was definitely not young. He had to be at least 40 years old and the fact that Mr Smithy had taught him surprised Daniel. "Wait, he taught you?"

"Of course. He has taught my family for generations."

"WHAT?" The whole class shouted.

"How old is he?" Kyla asked, her eyebrows raised with curiosity.

"I am actually not quite sure." The teacher replied. "Let's just say he is old."

"That's an understatement." Mackenzie muttered to Daniel and he smiled at her.

"Anyway." Monsieur Pris said, snapping the class back to attention. "We are getting off topic. Today's lesson will be in pairs and yes, you can choose who to work with. Keep in mind that a competition will take place so choose wisely."

Someone tapped Daniel roughly on the shoulder and he found Delvin, whose hair was sticking up more than usual. He grinned.

"Partners?" He asked and Daniel nodded. He was a bit disappointed though, having wanted to be Mackenzie's partner instead and wondering why she hadn't even asked him. Then, he caught sight of her at the back of the class with Ingrid, an evil smile on her lips and he realised that he knew the answer. He knew what she was planning.

Kyla was paired with Livia, whose pink eyeshadow matched the streaks in her hair and whose eyes sparkled with excitement. Kalen and Zilef were standing at the front of the class: Zilef was smiling happily but Kalen was frowning for some reason, a determined look in his eyes. Off to the far left of the room, Malcom was whispering to a tall, white and grey haired girl, who Kyla had told him was Zila- a girl who had the same twisted, cruel, unpleasant personality as Malcom. Malcom saw Daniel looking at them and he sneered at him until Monsieur Pris called for everyone to pay attention.

"Since you have all had a little practice with shapeshifting, we are going to see how accurate your animals actually are. The most accurate out of the pairs wins! Everyone stand in a circle around the platform! Come on, hurry up please!"

Everyone rushed forward in their pairs. Daniel and Delvin stood in between Kyla and Kalen and together they helped form a wide ring with all the other students. A smaller circle lay inside their ring and when Monsieur Pris pressed a button on his watch, the area inside the smaller ring sank and a cage raised itself out from within. Kyla nudged Daniel and he leaned forward to get a better view of the cage. Inside lay the most adorable puppy he had ever seen, with white fur and huge ocean blue eyes. He gave a small sneeze and the class dissolved into "Awww"s.

"Best person out of your pairs moves to the next round. You have thirty seconds. Go!"

The teacher began the timer and Daniel was so distracted

by the puppy's eyes that he noticed a second later. Delvin was already attempting to change his eyes from black to blue, so Daniel reached into his energy reserve and focused on the dog in front of him, memorising every detail.

He focused on the snow-like super soft fur. POP! He focused on the irises of a deep blue with a lighter sapphire shade sticking out at places. POP! He focused on the small round nose in the centre of its snout. POP!

Every detail morphed in Daniel's mind and before he knew it, everything was coming together.

"Times up!" Monsieur Pris shouted and some students protested about needing more time but the teacher shook his head and started to walk around the groups. "Malcom you pass- though only barely. I have to say, this is absolutely shocking. You had to turn into a dog. Not create a whole other species!"

Malcom turned back into himself and glared at the teacher before stomping over to the "safe" corner, whilst Zila stalked towards her desk having been eliminated.

"Mackenzie you pass. Sorry Ingrid, better luck next time. You did do better than Malcom though!"

Ingrid smiled. "That's not really reassuring but I'll take it!" She followed Zila's path to her desk and Mackenzie started doing a victory dance, moving her hips from side to side and waving her arms around. She grinned when she noticed the teacher's confused expression and walked over to where Malcom stood.

"Hmm not bad Mr Whixx, yes I think that you pass as well, very good job if I do say so myself. You and your sister look almost identical to the animal. You both clearly pass!" Monsieur Pris said.  Daniel looked back at his sister and, indeed, she looked like a replica of the puppy except she had gotten the eyes wrong making them purple instead of blue. He could tell his own eyes were a slightly darker colour too.

Since there were five pairs, Monsieur Pris randomly chose someone to automatically pass to the next round- the final. That person turned out to be Mackenzie. Kalen also managed to beat his partner but he didn't last long as he chose to go against Kyla, who, this time, perfectly matched the earthy turtle in front of them.

Which meant that Daniel was stuck with the only other person: Malcom.

"This should be easy." Malcom sneered, his back arched forward as he stalked next to Daniel.

"Did you seriously not pay attention to what Monsieur Pris said?" Daniel asked. Then he changed his voice to make it a few octaves lower. "I haven't seen such talent in generations."

"Whatever." he said angrily, glaring at him. Monsieur Pris started the timer and they both tried to turn into the falcon they were attempting to copy.  Daniel watched as his wings turned into the exact shade of colour that they needed while Malcom's grew to a miniature size, his beak smaller and less curved, his feathers brightly coloured and his eyes somehow a light shade of pink. Daniel let out a squeaky chirp.

"Well it is clear who won that round." Monsieur Pris said with a laugh. Malcom transformed back and scolded before he stormed out of the classroom. "We appear to have run out of time, so I will declare the winner from what I have seen."

"I wonder who won." Ingrid whispered as she stood next to Daniel.

"I already know." Zilef said, with a grin at both Daniel and Kyla.

"The winner, or should I say, winners are the twins!" The room erupted with congratulations as everyone cheered, apart from Zila who marched out of the room. Kyla and Daniel smiled at each other whilst their friends surrounded them and Monsieur Pris gave them his praise.

The teacher then went around complimenting or berating the students depending on how they had done. By the end of the lesson Daniel was ready to flop on his bed. But as he was heading back to his room with Ingrid and Zilef (Mackenzie had mysteriously declined Daniel's invite to join them) he overheard Ms Orgi talking to the principal. He stopped and slouched near the doorway straining to hear while Ingrid and Zilef hid behind him. He couldn't make out very much but was able to follow most of the argument.

"I'm telling you it's not normal. Someone purposely used a lot of dangerous animal DNA samples to create their creature." he heard Ms Orgi say. He peeked through the gap between the door and saw her pacing as Ms Smith sat behind her mahogany desk.

"Piper, calm down. Why don't you check all of their projects? I'm sure we can find out who it was." she replied, her hands folded over her desk.

"I did but no student used those DNAs in their project. That means that they were stolen by someone in this school. By one of the students here." she whispered nervously, her eyes flickering around the room.

"Ok. If it's one of the students then that means that the vials are still here in their rooms, so we should be able to find out who it is." Ms Smith was saying. But at that moment the opposite door crashed open. A guard stormed in, dressed in silver armour and a massive sword strapped to his back. He nodded at Ms Orgi before hurriedly talking to the principal.

"Ms, we have some bad news. An unauthorised drone has just left the school ground." he said.

"WHAT?" Ms Smith stood up quickly storming out of her office and following the guard down the corridor, Ms Orgi hot on her heels. Daniel transformed into a beetle and flew after them with Ingrid and Zilef copying him. Though Ingrid's wings were lopsided and Zilef had turned a weird shade of orange.

"When did this happen?" Ms Orgi asked as they raced through the school grounds.

"Just under 5 minutes ago on the roof of the north wing. We noticed a masked figure with it, though she fled when we tried to apprehend her." the guard explained now heading up a flight of stairs.

"She? How do you know it's a girl?" Ms Smith asked, pushing the trap door open and climbing onto the roof.

"Our analysis team analysed the footage taken by the security cameras just before they were disabled and were able to analyse the figure's body. It matches that of a girl." he said as they arrived on the roof.

Ms Orgi kneeled next to a lock of white hair and picked it

up. "What about this?" she asked.

"We think that is the hair from the perpetrator though the problem is that they could be shapeshifters so we can't be 100% sure that it's their real hair colour." the guard replied.

"If they can shape shift, how do you know their-" Ms Smith began before being interrupted.

"We've now stationed more cameras and added security systems to the school including…" Daniel didn't hear the rest of it as he flew back to the common area outside Kyla's house. He looked at Ingrid and Zilef who stared back at him, their eyes full of fear.

"Ok I guess we better tell Kyla what we learnt because I don't care what the grownups say. Adding more security isn't going to help the school. It's time we brought this into our own hands."

"It's time to find the mole.".

# CHAPTER 12

## KYLA

Lurking in the shadows at midnight was not how Kyla wanted to spend one of her last nights at school, before the winter holidays. Yet there she stood, crouched down next to Mackenzie, eyeing their surroundings. After a long discussion and debating, her friends had decided that they had to find the mole and Kyla was the first one on board the train 'to catch the thief.' She was now officially on the train 'to get her mom back' and nothing would stop her from reaching her destination.

Covered in black clothing and dirt, she was feeling the cold wind on her back and was silently thanking Mackenzie's suggestion of bringing a jumper. They stood below the trapdoor that led to the roof, waiting for Daniel and Kalen to arrive but with the darkness they could hardly see, even with night vision. Daniel had forced them to not shapeshift, saying that it'd 'ruin the fun'.

Mackenzie shifted and pressed her hand to her wrist, emitting a light. "Come in. Come in Red Panda. Are you guys on site?"

Silence. Then, "Yes we are Bald Uakari." Daniel's voice whispered through the wrist band.

"I told you not to call me that!" Mackenzie snapped. "Out of all the animals you have to choose that one for me. You couldn't have…"

Kyla pulled Mackenzie's wrist towards herself. "Focus." She hissed. "Red Panda, we're going out."

"Copy that Common Periwinkle." Her brother replied and she sighed. Why did she have to be called after a snail? Just because she had a periwinkle band did not mean she had to have it as a code name. Now she had the lamest undercover name ever.

She shook her head, trying to stay focused, and ushered Mackenzie forward. She motioned for Makenzie to lift her up but she shook her head, leaving Kyla to do the lifting. She hefted Mackenzie onto her back so that her friend would reach the trap door. Her back ached but she didn't move until Mackenzie lifted herself out onto the roof. Kyla reached up on her tippy toes and stretched her arms up for Mackenzie to grab, who pulled her up effortlessly.

"Bout time." Kyla jumped a good metre into the air as she spun to find two figures in front of her. A flashlight turned on and Kalen's face lit up. Daniel stood off to one side with Mackenzie, already looking around the roof. "Do you have your flashlight?"

"Of course."

She dug into her pocket and pulled out the torch, whilst Kalen gave his to Daniel. Together, Kyla and Kalen walked to the other side of the roof to look for clues. They only got a few steps to the right when Kyla lost her footing and tumbled to the ground with an "OW!". Her knee scraped the rough wood and a splinter dug into her flesh.

"Are you ok?" Kalen whispered as Makenzie glared at Kyla, telling her to "Shhhh!"

"I'm fine." She whispered back, accepting his reached out, gloved hand and getting back on her feet. Her glove scraped something next to her and she swung back to it, flashing her light down at the floor. "Kalen, look!"

She lent down, picking up the smooth, emerald, green fabric and handed it to him.

Kalen sucked in a breath. "Do you know what this is?" He

asked and when Kyla shook her head he continued. "It's the same fabric from the clothes of the Crocodiles, which means that…"

"How do you know?" Kyla interrupted.

"It has the same feel. Same texture as our own shirts. Feel it."

Now that Kyla really felt the fabric she agreed that it was just as smooth and light as their own Octopus' shirts and a sudden realisation hit her. "Then that means…"

But Kalen shook his head. "It doesn't mean anything. For all we know this might've been here for weeks!"

He was right of course and with each passing thought Kyla felt her shoulders slump. If this wasn't proof then how would they ever find the mole? How would they ever find their mom? It could take days, weeks, months. Maybe even years! Maybe by the time they had figured it all out their mom would be…

"Hey." Kalen told her, putting a halt to her spiralling thoughts. "Don't look so disheartened. There's an easy way to see how old this shirt really is. I just have to analyse it."

She snapped to attention. "Analyse it? You can do that?"

"Yep. And it'll only take around two days." He flashed a smug look. "The best part is we'll see the results together since you'll be staying with us over Christmas!"

"Can you guys stop having your little conversation for a second?" Mackenzie snapped from beside them. "Show us what you found." Kyla was about to pass the fabric over when Kalen snatched it from her grasp, claiming that they needed to keep it safe and not contaminate it with their fingerprints. But Kyla knew that he was just doing it to annoy Mackenzie and she couldn't quite cover her smile.

"And can I just say ugh." Mackenzie groaned as they made their way back to their huts. "As in ugh I have to stay with you guys for Christmas because my dad forced me to and I REALLY don't want to." Everyone glared at her and she shrugged. "What? Just wanted to lay it out there so you don't blame me if I get moody and ruin your festive spirit."

"Do shapeshifters celebrate Christmas in a different way?" Daniel wondered once they reached the campfire place and were nearing their homes.

"Nope. It's the same. We give presents and eat a big cake." Kalen replied. "Though there's no Santa Claus and I guess you've probably never had cake for Christmas have you?"

"Who has cake for Christmas?" Daniel asked. "That makes literally no sense.". Kalen laughed and they made their way to their rooms talking about the big Changeball game they had the next day.

They were still buzzing the next day by the time it was first period which unfortunately for them, had Mr Smithy.

He glared at all of them behind his sunglasses, his scowl plastered on his face.

"So it's the last class before term holidays" he started, studying each and every one of them in turn. "And I suppose this means as a teacher I should give you some presents" he mumbled whispering the last part.

"Pardon?" Ingrid called from her seat at the back. Mr Smithy and Mackenzie simultaneously glared at her.

"I said I'm going to give you presents! " he growled through gritted teeth, his jaw clenched so tightly it had to be painful. He snapped his fingers and an older student rushed in, his arms full of presents. He set them all down, his brown hair plastered to his forehead by sweat. Mr Smithy didn't even acknowledge or thank him, instead screaming for someone to hand them out which unfortunately led Mackenzie to grabbing all the presents and handing them out. She gave herself the biggest while Ingrid's was mysteriously misplaced. When she handed Kyla hers, she had a very smug look. Kyla tentatively opened the present expecting a horrible explosion but luckily all that was inside was a T- shirt that read: I live with this dumb stupid head followed by an embarrassing photo of Daniel. She couldn't help grinning at the twisted present and her grin grew when she saw Daniel had received a Falcons Changeball cap while Kalen had been given a baby anaconda as a pet. Though it faded when she saw that Mackenzie had been given a massive pranking kit which did not bode well for the class particularly Ingrid who had somehow managed to teleport to the other side of the room the moment Mackenzie had opened her present.

Unfortunately for them none of the other teachers gave them anything apart from homework for the holidays causing several people from the year to start speculating whether or not Mr Smithy had been an imposter. However these claims were squashed when they spotted him gleefully chasing after Mr Butland, who was attempting to get rid of his present, which had included a baby doll who screamed and acted like a real toddler would.

However, apart from that, the rest of the day was a blur as the entire school was buzzing for the game between the Oxen and the Octopuses for several reasons including the fact that Mackenzie had been named captain and as everyone knew she was a big cheat, this caused a lot of excitement for the game. She'd learnt that Zilef would be playing but was unsure of the rest as she was still super excited to make her debut. She also knew that Mackenzie had gone around taunting and mocking the Oxen, which did not bode well as when Kyla had run into her opponents, they had looked so angry that she was surprised that Mackenzie was still alive. When the clock chimed, the friends made their way to the changing room at 4 o'clock.

As they entered Kyla took in the beautiful changing room. The benches were arranged in a perfect circle with large, customised lockers right behind them with a photo of them. In the middle of the room there was a table full of snacks and refreshments while on the benches lay their purple kits.

Rhea stood waiting for them inside, and once everyone had walked in and started getting prepared she spoke.

"You might be wondering why our glorious captain is not here." She said sarcastically. "Well, Decker decided to go home early for Christmas. Had some important family business."

Mackenzie started to cheer and soon the whole squad followed. Rhea turned towards her and a slight smile seemed to be tugging on her lips.

"Ms Orgi found me and asked me to step in, so here I am." Kyla whistled and everyone started clapping for Rhea, who blushed, embarrassed. "Thank you. Now, let's get ready. Listen up!"

Kyla made her way to the locker allocated to her and picked up the kit with her name on it that lay nearby on the bench. She opened her locker and stepped inside as it transformed into a spacious wardrobe with various shoes, skirts, shirts and hair products. There was a ginormous mirror, which she used to look at herself when she had finished. She looked fiery in the short, two layered violet skirt and the fitted, sleeveless crop top that matched the skirt perfectly in colour. Her hair was tied in two perfect braids and she had chosen the white trainers to finish the look.

Rhea was still updating the team on her strategies for the game by the time everyone had gotten dressed and had sat down to hear the last instructions. All the girls were dressed the same as Kyla, with the kit and the two braids. The boys, on the other hand, wore purple shorts and fitted purple shirts. All kits had the swirling tentacles of the octopus curling from the back to the edges on the front of the shirts, whilst the bottom half of the kit was only purple.

"Photo everyone!" Rhea said and the whole team lined up in their positions. Daniel was in the middle in his yellow goalie kit with Kalen, and the older teammates: Trayton, Ashlin and

Zim right behind him, while Kyla and Skylar, another third year, were both on the sides. Mackenzie meanwhile lied down in the centre hogging most of the space. Again. Rhea pressed the button and raced into the space next to Mackenzie, who frowned and moved just an inch to the left before the camera flashed and the picture was taken.

"Good luck everyone!" Rhea shouted. "See you at half time! Go Octopuses!"

"Go Octopuses!" Everyone chorused.

The 8 players walked out on the pitch with Mackenzie leading the way as captain. She also made sure that they were all in the exact right order being Daniel, Kalen, Ashlin, Zim, Trayton, Kyla and Skylar. As they made their way onto the centre of the pitch Kyla could hear a familiar voice commentating.

"And here they come!" Ingrid's voice was saying. "By far the best house. And I am not being biassed! Mackenzie, the captain, is leading the line with a grin on her face. But how long will the grin last? I wonder. Tell me Malcom what do you make of the Octopuses chances today".

"I bet the Whixx twins are going to make a fool of themselves and the Octopuses will lose." The sneery voice said and Kyla clenched her fists. "But don't worry. I'm sure the Octopuses will keep smiling. Afterall, they are the Optimistic Octopuses." This led to a massive laugh from the stands and when she looked she noticed some of the teachers laughing as well.

Kyla watched as Zilef and Mackenzie shook hands and on the board, flashed a blue light, indicating that it was a passing bonus. Mackenzie grabbed the Warrall and waited for the whistle to blow. A few moments later the sharp squeal from the whistle cut through the air and the game began. Mackenzie passed the ball back to Ashlin and then to Kyla, who flew forward making herself have wings while she weaved and ducked past the Ox defenders. She then played it forward and Mackenzie bulldozed past the defenders, whipping the ball around and scoring the opener. In celebration, Mackenzie ran in front of the crowd sticking her tongue out and doing a rather obscene gesture at Ingrid and Malcom. She went back to the starting circle and smiled smugly at Kyla. The rest of the game was a blur to Kyla; she only remembered her 3 goals, Mackenzie's 5 goals which she bragged about afterwards endlessly and Daniel's incredible saves, which without them, they probably would have lost. Though it was a bit suspicious that his penalty save happened right after Mackenzie had stood up to Zilef leaving him scared and terrified. She made a mental note to check up on him and make sure he wasn't blaming himself for the loss. In the end they won 10-2 and Mackenzie led the celebrations in the changing rooms.

Ingrid's shouts of delight could be heard all the way from Kyla's locker and even when she locked the door she could keep hearing them. Rhea's shouts of joy were just as bad as she entered the changing room and congratulated them all. She brought snacks and soon everyone on the team was gobbling up the chocolate chip cookies, though Ashlin stated that she preferred the vanilla ones. Kyla chatted animatedly with Skylar about the match, right up until they reached her dorm and she had to wave goodbye to her new friend and Ashlin, who happened to be roommates.

She was about to enter when she heard a soft female voice speaking in the shadows nearby. She transformed into a fly and flew over to a dark corner. There she saw a hunched and hooded figure in the shadows. She flew over and hid near the figure in black listening closely to what she was saying.

"That's right boss, I'm in." the voice said in a familiar tone and volume. "Nah it was simple to get the things we need. I'm still working out a few things but it should be ready by the 2nd of June. And then we shall have our revenge." It said cackling as whoever the person was talking to responded. "And don't worry I'll watch the twins for you." Then Kyla heard a small, barely audible click and the next second the figure was gone.

Kyla was speechless. She barely breathed as she realised what she had just discovered. Because she knew who that voice belonged to.

It belonged to Zila.

# CHAPTER 13

# DANIEL

"Are you 100% sure it was Zila's voice?" asked Kalen for what had to be the 3,000th time that morning. Kyla had already told them about what she had heard last night and the others were shocked. Daniel's mind spun with what that meant.

"Yes I'm sure. I even found some of her hair in the corner." Kyla pulled out a sealed packet and they all stopped walking to take a closer look.

That morning they'd had to wake up extremely early for breakfast and now the five of them (Daniel, Kyla, Mackenzie, Kalen and Ingrid) stood outside the school gates, waiting for Ms Smith.

Mackenzie had boasted to the others that she had suspected Zila from the beginning although she clearly hadn't.

Unsurprisingly, she'd suspected Ingrid (which was probably the reason behind Ingrid's glares). Mackenzie had a lot to say about not having been invited to spy on the conversation but Kyla reminded her that she didn't know what was going on and barely had time to hide.

Mackenzie refused to accept this, however, and was sulking by the time Kalen's mom arrived to pick them up.

"Hey guys. Are you all excited for the holidays?" she asked, smiling at them and messing up Kalen's perfectly groomed hair which had taken him 23 minutes and 48 seconds to style. Yes, Daniel had counted. After all, there was no way he was losing a bet with Mackenzie.

They all attempted to sound enthusiastic but it seemed forced. Luckily Ms Smith assumed that they were exhausted from the Changeball game the day before and didn't say anything to them as she opened a portal to lead them to her home.

"Whoa. You live here?" Ingrid asked as she looked at the massive home before her. "It's beautiful!"

"You live in a palace and you find this beautiful?" Mackenzie scoffed, rolling her eyes at her.

Ingrid blushed and shifted uncomfortably. "It's still pretty." she mumbled.

"Thank you, Ingrid." Ms Smith smiled. "Oh and while we are here, I'd prefer we keep things as informal as possible so please call me Gwenda."

The friends nodded and Ms Smith- or Gwenda- dug out a rectangle gadget with a cobalt gemstone and azure swirls. She pressed it against the door and it clicked open.

"YOU'RE BACK!" A voice shrieked and a blonde tornado crashed towards them until it reached Kalen and gave him a hug. Kalen gently let go of his brother, and William turned to the others with a look of surprise.

He turned to his mom, a hint of pink rising in his cheeks. "I didn't know his friends were coming over."

"Does it matter? Do you have a problem with someone?" his mom asked him, raising an eyebrow, in a teasing way. William flushed pink and apologised before making his way to the kitchen for a snack.

Kalen grabbed the twins by the arms and pulled them forward, whilst Mackenzie and Ingrid raced to catch up. "I'll show you to your rooms."

"I'll bring extra clothes and mattresses. Room 5 and 7." Gwenda smiled and went left whilst Kalen led everyone else right and up the stairs. They climbed 3 sets of stairs and walked down the corridor for a few seconds until Kalen opened one of the rooms.

"Here we are. Girl's room." He said.

"Wait!" Mackenzie shouted. "Royal Lemon and I need to sleep in the same room? Ugh!"

"I feel the same way!" Ingrid snapped back.

The two fought back and forth and Kalen grimaced, looking at Kyla apologetically who looked extremely uncomfortable. "Sorry, it was my mom's idea."

"Don't worry." She smirked. "If they get annoying, I'll smack them with my pillow."

"Me too!" Daniel agreed and she nudged him hard, almost making him lose his footing. "Oh it's on!" It was lucky that Kalen led Daniel away towards their own room because they could hear the commotion of Ingrid refusing to be alone with Mackenzie, claiming she was going to prank her.

Kalen laughed and showed Daniel the room allocated for them over the holidays, which was MASSIVE! It resembled a small rainforest complete with real plants and vines.

"Wow how'd you do this?" he asked Kalen, fingering the super soft blanket lying on one of the bunk beds.

"Clever bit of shapeshifter magic from my dad. This is my lab. My escape from chaos." he said, laying his stuff on the middle bed. "My dad said that if we have bunk beds then the room that they're in should look like a rainforest since… I don't know. He thought it would look cool." he smiled.

Daniel grinned. It definitely looked cool. He made his way over to Kyla's room. He only had to take one step towards it, to hear Ingrid and Mackenzie's shouts slam into him. He poked his head in and was met by even louder screams. He made his way into the room and pulled the two of them apart.

"Alright break it up you two, calm down" he said standing between them. "We got more important stuff to discuss so for the good of the world put your differences apart for a couple of minutes, OK?" he glared at them until they nodded reluctantly.

"How come when you tell them to stop, they do it?" Kyla mumbled from where she lay with a pillow over her head. "I've been trying for five minutes straight!"

"You know why." Kalen said, striding into the room. Daniel turned towards him and Kalen winked, before turning serious. "Ok we have one small problem. Someone needs to keep my mom and William busy for the next couple of hours. Any ideas?"

"Ok. Kyla, go hang out with Will and get Ms Smith to make you a snack or something." Mackenzie said, gesturing at her to get lost. Kyla glared at her and Daniel could tell she was frustrated..

"Why me?" she moaned. "Why can't you do it?"

"Because William doesn't like me as much as he likes you. In fact he doesn't like me at all. And also for revenge for not taking me along yesterday on your little spy mission." she replied matter- of- factly.

"It wasn't a spy mission! It was… ugh, fine I'll go." She stormed out of the room and Daniel heard the stomps of her feet and her "William, want to play?" from all the way upstairs.

"Ok, so we need to do a bit of research as to what could happen on the 2nd of June. Then we have to figure out ways to tail Zila when we get back to school" Daniel said. He then divided the 4 of them into teams deciding it'd be best to put Mackenzie and Ingrid in opposite teams. He worked with Mackenzie while Kalen paired up with Ingrid. He then asked Kalen if they had a computer or a library to use to research. It turned out that he did have a library but Kalen told him to go to his secret lab instead since it would be more hidden and they wouldn't be disturbed.

Kalen turned towards his desk and ducked under it. A few beeps filled the room before a secret compartment revealed itself. Mackenzie gasped. Daniel looked into the dark hole uncertainty.

"Are you sure this is safe?" he asked.

"Don't worry there's a slide to help you down and you fall into a ball pit so that you don't get hurt." He said confidently. Daniel shrugged and jumped into the hole. He slid down and ended up crashing into a ball pit. He stood up and took in the massive sight before him. The lab itself was filled with all sorts of test tubes and tools. The gadgets around amazed him but he had absolutely no idea what any of them were or did. They looked like things that you would find in a spy lair, not what you would find in a thirteen-year-old's-secret-room.

Mackenzie crashed next to Daniel and together they got to work figuring out what was happening on the 2nd of June, whilst Kalen and Ingrid analysed the piece of fabric. They managed to discover that the annual Shapeshifter's summer show was on the day of the plan and the results showed that the cloak was from the crocodiles confirming their worst fears.

"I was hoping we were wrong about this." Kalen said that night as they made their way to dinner. He and Ingrid had decided to schedule patrols to follow Zila around school, though it'd be pretty hard to do so unnoticed.

The friends ate mostly in silence, not wanting to attract

Gwenda into their schemes. Daniel leaned back as he ate the last spaghetti on his plate.

"Wow Ms Smith, that dinner was delicious." Ingrid said politely once she had finished.

"Thank you Ingrid, you're so sweet to say so" she replied smiling. Mackenzie mimed gagging behind her and Daniel had to stifle a laugh. "Don't forget that tomorrow is Christmas." Ms Smith said as they went up to their rooms. Daniel thanked her and said goodbye to the others before flopping onto his bed. But as he drifted off to sleep he couldn't help but feel as if something about their investigation seemed off…

# CHAPTER 14

## KYLA

Kyla was dreaming peacefully when two hands suddenly grabbed her shoulders and she was shaken awake. Her eyes snapped open and they were met with two beautiful teal ones. Though they looked extremely angry. She only had to glance a bit upwards to guess why.

Ingrid's normally dark and straight hair was now bright pink and sticking out from all sides making her look as if she had shocked herself.

"Oh my. What happened to you?" Kyla asked horrified though she had a sinking feeling that she could guess.

"Someone, Mackenzie" She whispered to Kyla angrily. "Dyed my hair while I slept. She didn't even care whether it was Christmas or not." She was so angry that her eyes twitched.

"It's not that bad. Maybe I can fix it later. Wear this for now." Kyla said, passing her a pink cap of a similar shade of pink. But just as Kyla was looking around for something to help Ingrid further, Mackenzie stormed in, screaming at them to get downstairs for their Christmas presents. In fact, based on the looks of the rest of their friends it looked like she had woken all of them up herself. Kyla waved good morning while Ingrid adjusted her hat, glaring daggers at Mackenzie, who looked nicely brushed and tidy.

"Now to open presents!" Mackenzie said. She jumped up and down, clapping her hands in excitement.

"Couldn't we have done this later?" Kalen yawned.

"Better question." Daniel stepped in, looking over to where Ingrid stood, slouching. "Why are you wearing a hat?"

She slouched even more, which made Mackenzie howl with uncontrollable laughter. She laughed for two minutes straight, whilst Kalen and Daniel gave Kyla a confused look. She shook her head at them indicating for them to drop it. Daniel shrugged.

"Shouldn't someone wake up William?" Kyla asked, wondering how he had escaped Mackenzie's hurricane of doom.

"I'm here." he said and Kyla felt herself jump. She did not know he would be there though in her defence, he was hiding behind the couch, completely out of sight. She saw him crawl out from behind and stand up, beside his older brother. The two were splitting images. Both had the same, stripey, blue pyjamas. Both had their blonde and blue hair sticking up in all directions. Both had the type of expression one has when being woken up without their own consent, which was probably what had happened.

"Open presents?" Mackenzie asked.

"Fine by me." Another voice yawned and Kyla turned to see Gwenda slowly walking down the steps. She walked very slowly, which was due to her drooping eyelids and her having to constantly stop to smack her cheek, in order to stay awake. "Let me get my camera."

Kyla waited for Gwenda to pull out a phone-like device but she got a rubber duckie out instead. "All set." She mumbled. Daniel and Ingrid stared at her but decided to open the presents instead.

The six of them decided on an order for opening the presents. The order was: Mackenzie (though it wasn't much of a choice since she sat on the carpet and refused to move until all her gifts were opened), Daniel (who quickly copied

Mackenzie), Kalen, Ingrid, William and finally Kyla. She was actually thrilled with going last. Best for last, she always said.

Mackenzie had received pranking supplies from everyone and a MASSIVE present from Mr Smithy which turned out to be a Falcons poster, with glowing lights and a "The Jaguars will NEVER beat the Falcons!", which was a call back to their first ever conversation. It seemed pretty touching for Kyla, though Daniel clearly disagreed as he demanded that Mackenzie throw it out the window the second she got it out of the wrapping.

Daniel had opened up some new Changeball gloves and a couple of the Rhino's kits from his friends Lucas and Vasquez. He had also received a rather terrifying present from Mr Smithy labelled "exploding gas", with a disturbing picture, that Kyla refused to acknowledge.

Kalen had gotten a couple of action figures and a new Eagles scarf. Mackenzie had started laughing hysterically when he'd received it, stating that his room would look even more ridiculous. He glared at her and they started bickering (to no one's surprise), whilst Kyla and Daniel tried to break them up.

When it was Ingrid's turn, she adjusted her hat and nudged Kalen out of the way. She reached for a present but stopped halfway after seeing Mackenzie's evil grin. She reached for two more but stopped again due to Mackenzie's outburst of laughter, before finally settling on the biggest one. Ingrid narrowed her eyes at Mackenzie who turned expressionless and Kyla figured out why a second too late. A gigantic pie flew out of the box and smashed towards Ingrid but she dived at the last second. She grinned but Mackenzie just collapsed in giggles as her prank had hit someone else instead. Poor William's face was covered with creme, which he was trying to remove. He called for his mom, but Gwenda appeared to be asleep, curled up on the bottom step.

Next Ingrid opened Kyla's present: a bag full of hair accessories, which seemed crucial after today's prank. Daniel gave her a rhino's shirt, which she loved and Kalen gifted her a full set of Changeball coaching things like a whistle and a megaphone. The rest of their friends gave her tiny gifts and her family informed her that she would receive the rest of her presents at home. She got so many presents that you could tell she was royalty.

William received action figures on famous shapeshifters. He got one in particular (an old bearded man with very little hair which suspiciously resembled Mr Smithy) which Kalen begged for him to trade with him. William refused and his older brother started listing ways to make it up to him.

Finally, it was Kyla's turn. She opened up a huge present from Zilef first, which turned out to be a mega set of holograms. Her favourites were the super rare magical creature ones including a unicorn and a leprechaun. Next, she unboxed Mackenzie's gift, which was a multicoloured shirt with a huge "DECIDE!" at the top of the front and an "Eagles/ Falcons" below it. She flipped it over and laughed with the saying "I am officially a FALCON!". Kalen and other friends gave her more holograms, whilst Ingrid gave her a boot, which could transform into any shoe she wanted. Kyla loved it! Finally, Daniel gave her the biggest box of chocolate she had ever seen and she gave a chocolate to each of her friends, before taking two for herself.

After what seemed like hours of discussions about the gifts, Daniel suggested they play some Changeball outside which everyone agreed to. They decided to balance the teams out with Ingrid and William being on separate teams. In the end they decided to have Ingrid, Kalen and Mackenzie VS William, Daniel and Kyla. The score ended 4-5 with Kyla's team winning though there was a LOT of cheating from Mackenzie's team including: 1. Mackenzie punching Daniel in the stomach to get him out of the goal and for Kalen to score.

2. Ingrid having the ball ripped out of her hands again by Mackenzie, even though they were in the same team. 3. Mackenzie screamed, booed and threw dirt at Daniel during Kalen's penalty, which came from a spectacular dive from Mackenzie in the first place. Daniel saved it anyway, but it still wasn't fair! So it was a relief when Ms Smith called them in to get changed.

The girls raced up the stairs and into their room. Kyla got out of her sports clothes and put on a navy and white chequered squirt as well as a white, short sleeved blouse with multi coloured butterflies. Ingrid however was raging at her hair so much that Kyla felt bad and collected all the hair products available, to try to help. She tried straightening the hair, then curling it at the ends but the intense pink colour was still too much so she grabbed the hair spray and some hair glitter and got to work.

The end product was spectacular. Kyla could hear Mackenzie mutter "Rats!" under her breath and she saw her stalk away. Ingrid's hair was black at the top but towards the middle it was bright pink with a tint of black waving in and out. Curls had appeared at the bottom and the whole effect was gorgeous paired with her teal eyes.

Ingrid looked in the mirror, squealed and hugged Kyla.

"Thank you! Thank you! Thank you!"

"No problem." She replied. Opening her drawer she took out a black crop top jumper and some white shorts for Ingrid, who put them on in a flash then ran downstairs with Kyla close behind her.

"Wow." Gwenda breathed, her eyes wide. "Your hair… is amazing!" Kyla spotted Daniel staring at Ingrid though he quickly avoided his gaze when he saw Mackenzie's ice- cold glare. They were about to start eating lunch when suddenly a loud knock on the door interrupted them. Gwenda opened the door and Kyla turned around to see Ingrid's mom come into the room. She didn't know who screamed louder Ingrid… or surprisingly Mackenzie. Ingrid rushed to hug her mom while everyone turned to Mackenzie.

"What? I'm a big fan!" she said sullenly. "It's Madame Lemoine! Madame Lemoine!"

Ingrid's mom smiled. "It is. And Ingrid dear, what have you done to your hair?"

Mackenzie turned the same colour as her hair and mumbled an excuse before fleeing to the table and stuffing her face with eggs. Lunch was mostly uneventful which was a surprise considering that Mackenzie was at the table.

Gwenda cleared her throat and spoke to her children.

"Your father is stopping by today."

"He is?" Kalen and William asked simultaneously whilst Kyla and Daniel asked "Really?". Ingrid giggled and Mackenzie rolled her eyes at all of them.

"Yes he'll be coming in the afternoon and will be dining with us." she said, amused by their reactions.

"Isn't he busy?" William asked.

"Yeah but it's Christmas, so he managed to get some time away." Ms Smith replied.

The two brothers were extremely chipper and upbeat for the rest of the day even after Mackenzie pranked them and left them dripping from slime. Ms Smith had just announced dinner when the door swung open and the tall man Kyla had seen in the family pictures strode in laughing when his two sons tackled him. Now that they were next to each other Kyla could see the similarities even better. They had the same eyes, hair and jaw though while Kalen was quieter his father was loud and confident. He messed up Kalen's hair before making his way to the rest of the group shaking all of their hands repeating: "Hey I'm Kalen's dad Mr Smith, pleasure to meet you."

He sat down and dug into the food, talking to each of them and getting to everyone equally. He seemed extremely cool and relaxed, pretty much the opposite of Kalen. He laughed when he found out about Mackenzie's pranks and spent most of the night listening to her bragging.

"What exactly do you work as?" Daniel asked him. Kyla turned to face the man and was surprised she knew so little about him. She was aware that he worked at school, helping Ms Orgi but she still wasn't 100% sure what he did.

"I mostly work at your school, helping Ms Orgi around. I get most of the animals for her lessons and take care of them between classes. But outside of school I help rescue creatures in the wild and get them to sanctuaries to rehabilitate them." He explained. "I'm also really good at stopping any illegal animal trafficking." he added with a wink.

"Our dad has helped hundreds of animals and solved loads of cases." Kalen said proudly. "He's the best"

'Thanks K but you're a little biassed. And anyway I'm not able to solve this last case. Now that's complicated."

"What case?" Asked Kyla, leaning forward.

"It's…" Mr Smith stopped after seeing his wife's not-so-subtle shake of the head. "It's nothing really."

Kyla raised an eyebrow. She was not convinced and apparently neither were her friends.

"Sounds like it's something big." Mackenzie noted. She

narrowed her eyes as Mr Smith and Ms Smith shifted uncomfortably. Luckily for them the doorbell rang and Mr Smith, literally, sprung from his seat to open it. A familiar tall figure stepped into Kyla's view and she smiled because it was the cheery ginger and blonde streaked man from a few months ago. The first shapeshifter they had met, apart from themselves.

"Icarus!" The twins shouted.

"Kyla! Daniel!" He enveloped them in a crushing hug, lifting them up and spinning them around. "I haven't seen you guys since you started school. How are you doing?" he messed up their hair and then nodded at their friends.

"We're good." Lied Kyla as she remembered her worries connecting to her mom. She shook her head and put on a fake smile. "What have you been doing all this time?"

"That's classified." He said then his face fell. "I'm sorry I'd tell you if I could. I swear! But I'm not allowed. I'm really sorry."

"That's ok." Daniel said, with a side glance at Kyla that seemed to say "we'll find out soon enough."

Mackenzie meanwhile was grumbling about all the people that were suddenly occupying the room.

"If one more person interrupts me while I'm having

dessert I'm gonna--" she didn't even have time to finish before the doorbell rang again. Quick as a flash Mackenzie got up and opened the door screaming "WHAT NOW??!!!" at the top of her lungs before gasping when she realised who it was.

"Dad?" she asked as Julius walked into the crowded room. "What are you doing here?"

"How nice to see you too Mackenzie." he said sarcastically before wrapping his arms around her. "I had to discuss a couple of things so I thought I'd come over to see you. How are you all?" he explained. He had barely sat down before the rest of the parents asked to meet in the office upstairs. The children rose to go but were ordered to bed. Kyla lay on her bed wondering what they were talking about up until Mackenzie's voice sliced through the silence.

"We're going to go stand close enough to hear everything right?" she asked.

"Mackenzie!" Kyla gasped.

"What? Aren't you curious?" She asked and Kyla had to admit that she was feeling the same way but it was still rude to overhear a conversation, which they had been told not to listen to.

"It could be important!" Mackenzie insisted.

"I'm sorry Kyla but I'm with Mackenzie on this one. I think we should eavesdrop." Ingrid whispered with a look of utmost disgust at the words she had just said. Mackenzie looked smugly at Kyla and she sighed.

"All right let's go" she said reluctantly, sneaking out of the door. The three stopped near the door, straining to hear through the walls.

"The disappearances are increasing. I don't know what to do. I swear my analyst team and I have been looking at every angle of the crimes but there's no clues left" Mr Smith was saying. "And there's no repetitive pattern either so there's no telling what will go missing next."

Icarus spoke next. "I tried searching for similarities in this crime and to some previous ones but I couldn't find any which only makes me think that they are connected even more. There's no way to track them either, all our technology has been disabled."

"I thought they could only be disabled from the inside?" Ms Smith asked, sounding confused.

"They must've done it somehow. Maybe through a spy." Icarus replied. Kyla, Mackenzie and Ingrid shared a look. They thought there was a mole at school, so if the grownups thought so too then there had to be one. And it had to be the same one didn't it?

"What happened after the last kidnapping?" Ms Smith asked.

"If I hadn't managed to get there when I did, a lot of bad info would be known right now. Classified information including some stuff about you know what" Icarus continued.

"But that's impossible, only people with high level clearance would have had access to it. What about the people who worked in the archives?" Ms Smith asked.

"Many employers quit after that." Julius said. "Some said it was stressful, others just left."

"You think one of them was a spy?" Ms Smith queried.

"Undoubtedly."

The girls eyed each other again. Kyla couldn't help wondering what this could mean. If they could get the adults to open up and share what pieces of evidence they had gathered then they could work together and find the mole once and for all. Mackenzie shook her head as if she had read Kyla's mind and the three of them retreated back to their bedroom. Kyla replayed what they had heard and drifted off to sleep knowing that this investigation had just gotten a whole lot more important.

# CHAPTER 15

# DANIEL

The rest of the holidays passed through quickly. Ingrid left, they played Changeball, went to the beach, played Changeball some more and before he knew it they were back in school.

"Those holidays flew by didn't they?" Kyla said to Daniel as they exited the rainbow portal that had transported them back to the common area in the yard, right next to the remains of what had to be a late-night bonfire.

"They did and yet we didn't accomplish anything did we?" Daniel sulked. "We still don't know who the mole is." Kyla opened her mouth but Daniel interrupted. "We don't know for sure that it's Zilla. Therefore we don't know who the mole is. We don't know who has taken the animals. We don't know who or why they took mom."

"Who took mom?" asked Kyla with a look of confusion and pain.

Daniel gulped. He hadn't meant to tell her his thoughts so early on but now he figured he had better spill his suspicions.

"Don't you get it? It's too much of a coincidence, isn't it? The same week that our house gets attacked, our mom vanishes and the creatures start disappearing. The same week."

Kyla blinked. "Are you saying the two might be connected?"

"It links and it gives us a clearer timeline of when the mole's plans started off."

"But we saw our mom's kidnappers. None of them were children like us."

Daniel raised an eyebrow. "Did we see them?" He paused letting his sister think about it. "Didn't we just hear their voices?"

"Ok but why is the mole here at school? There has to be something that we're missing. Why would they put themselves in danger like that?"

"Aren't you forgetting something?" Kalen interrupted, making both of the twins jump so high that they scared an innocent bird. Kyla even gave a little shriek. Honestly, Daniel had forgotten about Kalen and Mackenzie's presence.

"We analysed the fabric. The one we found from the roof." Kalen continued. "It was from the Crocodiles."

"We know." Kyla said, recovering from her earlier shock. "But we shouldn't let this blind us. Afterall, someone could've stolen the Crocodile's jacket to frame them. Throw everyone off their scent."

Daniel sighed. "This is getting us nowhere." He looked down at his watch. "It's almost 8:00 and I'm starving."

They made their way to the cafeteria and sat down at their usual table talking in hushed tones to make sure no one overheard them. Mackenzie glared as Ingrid sat down next to them but was quickly elbowed by Kyla.

"So what's going on that has you guys whispering?" Ingrid asked. "By this time, Mackenzie would have slung a couple of insults my way."

"Yeah I was sure that Ingrid would have had some yoghurt in her hair by now" said Delvin, making the others jump.

Man that guy is quiet. Daniel thought angrily just as Zilef took the seat next to him.

"How was your holiday?" Zilef asked but Ingrid interrupted him though not in a mean way.

"Not now! These four are acting suspicious." She glared at

them, and everyone looked away guiltily apart from Mackenzie who smirked. Daniel saw Kyla narrow her eyes at Ingrid and blink her left eye repeatedly as if trying to give her a silent hint, but Ingrid wouldn't get the gist. Zilef and Delvin leaned in too.

When the twins, Kalen and Mackenzie turned to look at each other, Zilef laughed. "What is up with you guys?" He looked at Kyla, but she looked away.

Finally, Daniel gave in. "Okay fine. There have been some suspicious things going on and we've been trying to figure out who's behind it."

He looked at Kyla and they both started to explain everything. Right from their mother's kidnapping, up until the conversation that they'd heard last night. Kalen and Mackenzie joined in, giving any relevant details that they had missed until they had recounted every last detail. When they had finished Daniel breathed a sigh of relief and his chest felt a lot lighter now that they had no more secrets between their friends.

"We've been trying to find the mole all this time." He concluded.

"What?" Delvin asked, his face going ghostly pale.

"Are you guys sure?" Zilef asked "How do you even

know?”

“We overheard the principal talking about it. They saw this drone pick something up a couple months ago so we know it's a student because only the students can get that kind of technology past the front gate.” Mackenzie explained.

Daniel wasn’t sure how it was possible but Delvin went even paler.

“What's wrong with you?” Zilef asked.

“My dad got killed by a mole when he was working for the government” he whispered his eyes scanning the cafeteria suspiciously.  Kyla frowned and patted him on the back in comfort, whilst Daniel turned and gave Zilef a look of disgust. He nudged his chin in the direction of Delvin in what he hoped was a clear sign of apologise.

“Oh. My bad.” Zilef said, lowering his eyes. There was a tense moment of silence in which Zilef looked really uncomfortable and regretful.

“How much do you guys know about the mole?” Ingrid asked, breaking the silence.

“Well the principal doesn’t know this but we found some crocodile fabric where the drone was being picked up and the hair on the scene matches Zila.” Kalen said.

“But that could have been faked right? Anyone could have

gotten those things." Delvin said, looking at Daniel apologetically. He had just added yet another flaw to their reasoning.

"True but she also had this." Mackenzie said, taking out a broken black piece of metal.

Kalen, Kyla and Daniel gasped but Delvin and Zilef looked unimpressed.

"A broken piece of metal? What good is that going to be?" Delvin said dismissively.

Kyla recovered first. "How'd you get that? Where did you…"

"It was in Zila's room."

"How'd you get in there? Without anyone seeing you?" Kalen asked.

She shrugged. "I'm a shapeshifter. It's what we do."

"Ok. You have got to teach me your ways!" Daniel exclaimed, fist bumping her.

"It's got to be her then." Zilef concluded and then he shouted "CASE CLOSED!"

Everyone's head in the cafeteria turned towards them and Kyla hushed Zilef and told him to sit back down. Delvin still looked unconvinced.

"That could have been placed there; it's not hard to break

into other people's rooms." He insisted before realising what he had said and looking down at his feet.

Mackenzie leaned in aggressively. "How do you know that?"

Everyone ignored her.

"You're right but then who is it?" Kyla mumbled, pulling out strands of hair, which was another one of her nervous habits.

"I think it could be…" He paused. "So during the holidays I took a drama improv class and did a lot of gardening. It was really awesome." Delvin replied loudly. Daniel raised his eyebrows extremely confused until they all turned and saw Mr Smithy breathing down on their necks. His pointy nose inches away from stabbing Daniel in the forehead.

"An improv class? You know I myself dabbled in the performing arts department though my talent was never uncovered. A real tragedy. I could always do happy, sad, frightened but never deranged." he said.

Daniel coughed loudly.

"Are you alright there Mr Whixx?" The teacher glared at him. "Anyway you must get me the name of your drama teacher, perhaps he can help me…yes...yes…yes" he rambled looking off into space. Vasquez cleared his throat from across the cafeteria and the teacher quickly snapped back to attention before leaving on his scooter.

"A drama class? Gardening?" Mackenzie scoffed.

"What? I like those stuff, they soothe me, plus they're good skills to learn especially if-" Delvin began before going quiet.

"What is it?" Daniel asked.

"I just saw Ms Smith going on to that stage over there." he said pointing. Daniel turned around and saw Kalen's mom making her way up to a massive stage which now took over the majority of the cafeteria causing the other tables to end up squashed on the sides.

"Hello everyone! I hope you've all had a restful and well-earned break from school because I have some incredible news for you. Our school has been selected to host this year's New Moon Festival!" she shouted excitedly. The room exploded in cheers as the students screamed in joy at this revelation.

"What's the New Moon festival?" Daniel asked over the loud clamour of students.

"It's this incredible celebration that happens annually at a different location. Many millennia ago our world Ocelia was dying, we had no food, no water and no supplies. The species were at war with each other and the extinction of our species was close. However one day a huge comet got pulled into our planet's atmosphere. As you know the gravity from our planet is much stronger than most so the comet turned into our 3rd moon. When it passed it caused our plants to grow to heights and lengths unlike anything we'd ever seen and our rivers were full of water once again. This helped stop the fight and to commemorate it the leaders of the 5 kingdoms came together to put in place new laws and rules." Zilef explained in his lecture voice. He started making an image with his food to illustrate the different parts of the world.

"As you know Ocelia is divided by several kingdoms: the fairies and dragons, the ogres and trolls, the animals, the gnomes and goblins, and us shapeshifters. These divisions have allowed our world to stay safe since the fight, but every year the leaders come together and host the New Moon festival to celebrate the creation of Ocelia and allow our different species to combine and create new memories together." He finished.

"That's cool." Kyla said.

But Daniel's thoughts were spinning so fast that he could hardly focus on all of them. An event so important…With so many people…

"When is this festival?" He asked and he closed his eyes, praying for a different answer from the one that he knew was coming but his wish was not granted as Zilef unveiled the answer.

"June 2nd.".

# CHAPTER 16

# KYLA

"Kyla quick. You have to see this!"

Mackenzie's shout came from inside their dorm but Kyla was too busy talking to Kalen about Changeball practice and the extra support she could give him.

"All you need is confidence." She was saying before she was so rudely interrupted. "How about we play after lunch? With Daniel and maybe Mackenzie."

"Not Mackenzie." Kalen shook his head vigorously. "She'll laugh at me."

"No she won't." Kyla said but then she had to admit that it was extremely likely. Mackenzie would tease everyone but the fact that she seemed to loathe Kalen made it worse for him. "Look, we can-"

"KYLA COME!!!" Mackenzie shrieked at the top of her

lungs from somewhere inside.

Kyla rolled her eyes and excused herself as she raced inside, following the sound of her roommate's shouts until she arrived outside of her own room. The door was left open and Kyla could see that she was kneeling on her purple carpet, holding something in her hands. She also appeared to be laughing until Kyla stepped closer and saw that she was actually crying.

"What's wrong?"

"LOOK!" Mackenzie turned around and thrusted her hands towards Kyla, who gasped and then shouted "awwww". Rested on her hands was an adorable little creature. It resembled a panther with dark purple fur that glowed with lighter purple patches. Its back had a big shark fin coming out from it and when the creature yawned Kyla got the glimpse of snake fangs growing out.

"What's wrong?" Kyla repeated as now she really couldn't tell what was wrong.

"I told Gabbi I didn't want it." She wailed.

"But why?"

"Because it's EVIL! Just look at it's EYES!" She held up the baby cub and Kyla leant forward, only to completely melt due to the cuteness in front of her. Those huge violet eyes just gleamed with cuteness.

"STOP BEING SUCKED IN BY ITS EYES!" Mackenzie shrieked. Just then Kalen rushed into the room too.

"What the-" He said before his eyes met the baby cubs, he gave an excited squeal and he leant forward to strangle-hug it.

"WHAT IS THIS CUTIE?"

"Hands off Princess Orchid you creep!" Mackenzie lunged forward and stole her creature out of Kalen's hands as both Kalen and Kyla asked "Princess Orchid?"

"I wonder if I got mine delivered..." With that, Kalen said goodbye to Kyla, ignored Mackenzie and rushed off, probably to find Daniel and then go to their dorm to check for his creature.

"Oh. Maybe you have yours in your room." Mackenzie thought and the both of them exited the room and went to Kyla's in search of her adorable companion.

And they found her.

Roxy, as Kyla called her, was curled up on her canopy bed, sleeping on an aqua pillow, purring softly. Kyla wasn't surprised to find her sleeping under a photo of a cheetah family as the tiny creature was part cheetah with its soft white cheetah print fur and tiny clawed hands. Wings sprouted from either side of its body of a light sky-blue colour the same colour as the patches on her fur. A scorpion tail curled outwards and a unicorn horn sprouted from its forehead.

It purred and opened its eyes which sparkled like the ocean on a summer day. Kyla rushed over and grabbed the little creature which continued purring, putting its tiny paws on her face. She ran to the cafeteria where she was instantly greeted by a barrage of screams and chaos. Everywhere she looked baby creatures were wreaking havoc on the poor older students while their creators attempted to control them.

"Watch out!" Daniel shouted as a small red animal whizzed past her. He was sweating and had a treat in his hand in an attempt to lure the creature towards him.

"C'mon Pyro get here right now!" he shouted.

Kyla looked at the little creature which roughly resembled a lizard. It was on its hind legs and had a Spinosaurus sail on its back with a large ankylosaurus tail. The creature's body was scaly but red with some occasional black and white spots from the panda DNA. Its head resembled that of a velociraptor and it had small bat wings on either side of its sail. It turned its small head and narrowed its emerald green eyes at Daniel before flying towards him and biting his arm.

"Ingrid, get him off me!" he shouted as he waved his arm

around widely in an attempt to shake it off before a shrill whistle sliced through the chaos. They turned and saw Ms Orgi with a whistle and multiple objects standing in the doorway.

"Ok everyone, normally you would have your lessons today but seeing how your animals are behaving we have decided to merge classes and so we'll have weaponry alongside our magical creatures' class." she said as Mr Alpesh stepped up behind her. For someone whose name meant small he was huge. He had light brown skin and short black hair. He smiled at the students, most of whom were still fighting their animals.

"Ok settle down everyone. Settle down."

A loud whistle cut him off and all of a sudden the animals shushed up. Kyla turned and saw Zila with her hand in her mouth having just blown the whistle that turned all the chaos into order. All the creatures stood with very straight backs, chins raised.

"Thank you Zila." Mr Alpesh said. "You have a marvellous way with animals."

Just like the mole… Kyla realised. Yet another fact and evidence that supported the theory of Zila being the mole! The sign was there! Stealing animals from their shelters could not be easy so of course the mole had to be great with animals, otherwise the commotion would surely give them away. Instead of causing panic, if they were highly trained with animals then they'd know how to calm them down and no noise would be made. No alert of an intrusion and capture would arise.

It all made sense! Delvin was wrong. It had to be Zila. It was Zila. Kyla was sure of it! But they now needed to prove it. They needed real, hard, cold evidence. They needed to set a trap...

"Kyla!" Kyla blinked, her thoughts coming to a halt. Kalen nudged her again and she turned to him.

"What's wrong?" He asked her but she shook her head.

"I'll tell you later."

She didn't have time to explain as she was told to join a table in the corner with Mackenzie, whilst Kalen was sent to another with Daniel. She pulled out a chair and sat fidgeting with the loose string of her skirt as her thoughts kept trailing back to Zila.

"Oh no." Mackenzie mumbled and a second later, the chair next to Kyla was pushed back and Zila sat on it. Her evil smirk turned in Kyla's direction and she laughed.

"What's with you today? Staring into space?" Zila sneered.

"Miss your mommy?"

Anger boiled in Kyla's stomach and she clenched her fists, growling. "Shut up!"

"Aw. I'm sorry. It's hard thinking of her being lost."

"Shut up!"

"Of her being trapped, hopeless…"

"SHUT UP!!!" Kyla screamed and threw herself onto the monster in front of her, her vision red with hate. She morphed into a tiger, clawing at Zila's exposed skin until she thrashed and flailed underneath her. Someone tried to get Kyla off of the girl but she stayed on, clawing and clawing, until a gentle hand rested on her shoulder and she could see clearly again. She looked up and saw Mr Alpesh grabbing her by the shoulder. His eyes stared deeply into hers and he shook his head. He led her over to Daniel's table and then went back to Zila, who had small bleeding scratches on her arms. Kyla couldn't help feeling satisfied with what she had done.

How dare she?

She sat back down and began to grab the tools she needed to create the transfiddler., her mind wandering back to her fight. She never got aggressive but Zila's smirk, her mocking voice, the fact that she knew, unleashed a beast from inside of her.

Kyla looked up and found that Daniel and Kalen were staring at her while Mackenzie nodded behind them clearly proud of her. Kyla glared at Mackenzie but she merely grinned back and gave her a thumbs up.

"What was that?" Kalen whispered. His eyes met hers and Kyla looked away, not prepared to explain.

"I'll tell you later." She hissed and started to turn away but Daniel grabbed her arm.

"Tell us now."

And she told them. Imitating Zila's smirks, smiles, grins and mocking voice. At the end of her lengthy dialogue Kalen was bad mouthing the girl, whilst Daniel sat silent.

"She was just being a bully." Kalen said after rambling on how much he hated those people. "You should've ignored her."

Daniel turned towards him, a look of absolute anger. "Don't you get it? She knew!"

Kyla had never seen Daniel so enraged in her life but now he looked ready to explode as he scanned the cafeteria for Zila.

"The event of the capture is classified, remember?" Daniel spat out.

"Only the kidnappers are meant to know about the attack,

no one else." Kyla explained. Kalen ran a hand through his hair and let out a weary sigh. He looked up at the ceiling for a couple of seconds before glancing at Zila and nodding his head.

"All right then, I guess we know who it is now," he said.

"Then that means we need to set a trap for her" Mackenzie whispered from behind them. The others looked at her in surprise. Whether it was for how she had creeped up so quietly or for the fact that she actually had a plan for once.

"What?" she asked suspiciously, noticing their confused faces.

"How on Ocelia are we going to set a trap?" Kalen asked with a raised eyebrow and Kyla immediately understood the change of how on earth to how on Ocelia.

Shapeshifters and their sayings…

"Easy." Mackenzie grinned.

"You're talking to the master trap setter."

# CHAPTER 17

# DANIEL

The days passed like a blur. Because between Changeball, training their creatures and other classes Daniel barely had time to relax. Even with the little free time he had, he put into setting the trap for Zila.

"This trap has to be perfect and who better than me to set it, right?" Mackenzie had said. Since then the four of them, Zilef, Ingrid and Delvin had begun creating the elusive plot that would hopefully capture the mole.

Daniel reflected on the plan as he made his way to his room. His head was still struggling to wrap itself around Mackenzie's plan. Not only was it incredibly complex but also devious. Just like Mackenize he thought to himself as he opened the door. But inside he found Mackenzie and Kyla both sitting on his bed talking to Kalen, Zilef, Delvin and

Ingrid.

"Oh hey guys, what are you doing here?" Daniel asked.

"We're talking about the plan for the mole duh" Mackenzie said with disdain. "Hey, is this your transfiddler for weaponry class?" She asked, holding the messy and half made weapon. Daniel glared at her and snatched it from her grasp.

"Cut me a break, Ms Hinkle gives so much homework I've barely had time to get started" he complained thinking of the short ruby haired teacher. "What about the plan? I thought it was perfect." Daniel replied, placing the machine back on the table where there was a mile high pile of sketches and drawings. He flopped onto his chair and stared at the faces staring back at him. Kyla looked determined, Kalen apprehensive, Mackenzie and Ingrid excited, Zilef seemed dejected and Delvin… it was difficult to describe almost as if he was wrestling with his true feelings.

"That's the problem. It's supposedly perfect, but how are you going to know if it is?" Zilef commented. "There are so many variables and ways it could go wrong. Not to mention it takes place on the 2nd of June. If we don't get it right their plan will succeed."

Daniel stared at his feet rather than at the people around

him. He sighed and ran a dejected hand through his long, crazy hair.

"We don't have time to change it, the festival is in 3 weeks there's no way anything else will work." Daniel explained, frustrated. "Look, I understand you may have some reservations on it but it can still work 100%" he continued. He scanned their faces once again and Zilef nodded.

"Wait, did he just say reservations?" Kyla asked, with a look of complete and utter shock. "Where'd you learn that word? Have you been reading?!"

"Nah. Monsieur Pris makes us learn new words in detention." Mackenzie whispered and Kyla opened her mouth, probably to lecture them again about behaving in school but luckily Ingrid interrupted, redirecting their conversation back to the trap.

"When should we start?"

"Right now!"

***

Daniel, Ingrid and Delvin flew to the library. Though Daniel had trouble focusing since being a fly meant you had like a gazillion more lenses than humans making it hard to remain concentrated on one object. He stopped just before the library door and transformed watching as Ingrid clutched her head.

"Remind me never to be a fly again" she said looking rather nauseous. Delvin looked at her surprised.

"Really? C'mon it's not that hard." he said. Daniel glared at him, thinking that he'd probably been practising turning into a fly. Afterall, it'd be harder to hit a fly in a battle and that was the way Delvin fought in Mr Smithy's class. In fact he was so bad at fighting Mr Smithy repeatedly gave him Z's and called him the foot of the class. Not the bottom of the class. The foot of the class. Humiliating.

"It's good for camouflage." Daniel added so that Ingrid would feel better. The less people that saw them the better. Daniel opened the library door and they went up to the librarian.

"Um.. Hi Ms Newta we need to borrow: Magical Herbs and their Effects please." Ingrid said, extremely politely. Ms Newta squinted at them suspiciously.

"Oh hello Ms Lemoine, yes you can borrow the book, however I must ask that you handle it with complete care, you see I lost a copy of the book earlier this year so I had to order this one. Do try not to damage it." she replied apprehensively.

"Don't worry, we'll be careful," Daniel commented confidently. He grabbed the book and they made their way back to his room where Mackenzie had returned from her own mission. She sat down excitedly and began putting different seed packets on the ground in a circle around her.

"Ok, if we want to catch Zila we need to read on how to set up trapper plants." she started quickly grabbing the book and flipping over the multiple pages. "The bad thing is that these plants are weak alone so we need to garden a large area in time for the second of June."

"Why not use this? If we do, it can make the plants stronger." Zilef asked, pointing to the page Mackenzie had opened on while looking for the instructions.

"The Moonstone Herb. A special type of plant capable of granting health and power to whoever uses it." Kalen read. He looked at Mackenzie who had gone red in anger.

"Because those plants only grow on the day of the festival. The light from the 3rd moon allows it to photosynthesise so it can create the sugar it needs." She explained. "Besides, only someone with master gardening skills could pull it off, so even if our trap was set for later, the instructions are notoriously difficult."

Daniel looked at the instructions again and he had to admit

it did look hard.

"Wait Delvin, you took a gardening class over winter? Couldn't you grow it?" Daniel asked. Delvin went pale and began sweating profusely.

"Well.. you see… I… it's too difficult" he stammered. His eyes dropped to his hands embarrassed and Daniel decided to drop the topic. He looked at Mackenzie and saw she was already getting to work on the plant. Since the instructions said the trapper plant could be grown and moved to different locations they decided to use Daniel's room for the time being and it soon became their base of operations. Mackenzie spent the majority of the time now planting which while some people found it a relief (Ingrid) Daniel thought it was depressing that she was using her time to help him. In fact he barely even got to see her apart from some moments where she told him to go away leading to him spending his day training for battle and working on the transfiddler. But no matter how much he tried he just couldn't get the cube to turn into other weapons. Basically… his life was deteriorating. It wasn't until a couple days later that he finally knew what he had to do.

Daniel stood watching Pyro poke his eyes with his little claws before squealing and looking up at him surprised.

"If you don't want it to hurt maybe you should stop doing that" he told the little lizard patiently. The creature snorted before flapping its tiny wings together and landing on his head scratching and pulling at his long hair. Daniel smiled sadly thinking of what would happen to Pyro if they failed.

"Hey are you ok?" a voice asked from behind Daniel in the middle of a magical creatures'class. He turned and found Gabbi staring at him. "What's wrong? You've been standing there for ten minutes while Pyro has been attempting to bite the other creatures and you haven't so much as scolded him" he looked at her large brown eyes and shook his head dejectedly. She stood next to him and leaned on to the wall behind her.

"Listen I'm not sure what is happening with you but whatever it is you have to snap out of it. You've been in a horrible, bored state for almost two weeks now and you're beginning to worry us." she continued.

"Us?" Daniel asked, raising an eyebrow.

"Yes, us. Lukas, Vazquez, Livia and I. We may not be part of your group as much but even I can tell something is up." she continued to stare at him until he relented.

"Ok fine. I'm worried about some…stuff and I don't know what to do. So many people are involving themselves when it's really my problem. I know they're trying to help but because of this they end up sacrificing their time for me when they could be doing whatever they want." he confessed, staring at where Pyro had begun ramming his little head into the wall, growling in surprise when he bounced off. He fidgeted with his uniform and looked at his boots.

"Listen, I don't know what you're going through, I don't know how you're feeling, but what I do know is get over it. People want to help you right? How is that a bad thing? Heck I wish my friends offered to help me out when I had problems." she replied. Daniel turned to look at her, then gazed at Pyro who had flown down to his feet.

"I'm not going to do some long winded speech about what's important or not, trust me I think you're smart enough to think of that. But I am going to say WAKE UP or I will channel my inner Mackenzie and make your life miserable". Daniel turned back to her and nodded, smiling.

"Thanks, that's just what I needed." he whispered gratefully while Pyro perched on his shoulder and screamed like a victor.

Daniel now knew what he had to do.

***

Daniel entered his room and found Kyla, Kalen and Mackenzie already sat on the floor talking, each of them looking worse than the other. He took a chair and gazed at each of them in turn.

"Guys we need to talk," he began. The others turned to him, surprised but subdued. "This isn't working."

"We know but what's there to do?" Kyla agreed. She sat twirling her hair into a fresh new braid, grey shadows under her eyes.

"We need to work together." Daniel said.

"We are." Kalen pointed out, meeting Daniel's eyes.

"No. We need to actually work together. Not 'each does one section of the plan' but we should actually work in pairs or groups. Never alone! These past few days have shown people, like Gabbi, that something's wrong."

"So?" Mackenzie asked boldly.

"So, the mole might see our changed attitude and realise we're onto them."

"He's right." Kyla turned to Mackenzie. "Didn't you notice Zila stare at us for far too long? Even after we saw her staring?"

Mackenzie gasped and growled. "She knows!"

"Maybe not yet. I mean everyone has a rough week. This can be ours. We just need to change and make up a likely story of why we are moody."

"Yes." Daniel said, with a clap of his hands. "From now on we will divide into pairs. Kyla and Mackenzie. Kalen with me."

"Sounds great," said Kyla with a smile. "Mac and I will work on testing the soil to figure out where we plant it."

"Did she just call me Mac?"

Kyla squirmed under Mackenzie's glare. "Nickname? You don't like it? I can change it."

"I actually like it." She grinned, then realised that Kalen and Daniel were both gaping at her. Who was this girl and what had she done with Moody Mackenzie?

She cleared her throat. "Carry on."

"You two just need to make sure that Zila doesn't suspect a thing."

But little did they know that the mole did suspect them… and they had a plan. A plan to destroy the school. A plan to destroy Ocelia.

A plan to destroy the twins…

# CHAPTER 18

## KYLA

The day had arrived. The day their plan would be set into motion. Kyla could feel the anticipation building deep within her. It all came down to this. She fidgeted with her uniform as Mr Butland, their intelligent but horribly boring history teacher, was wrapping up the lesson. His totally bald head gleamed in the soft glow of the room and his light blue eyes scanned the room until there was complete silence.

"Sometimes being spontaneous can save your life out in the field" he began, his eyes still scanning the classroom attentively. "Even the best, most thought out plans can fail, which is why it is important to always have something up your sleeve and never let them know your next move." he finished before rambling on about how it had helped him in a war 30 years ago.

Kyla looked around the class at her friends and saw her fear and worry reflected in their eyes. What if their most thought out plan failed? She turned back to Mr Butland trying her hardest to listen but every couple of minutes her mind would wander and she'd be thinking of their plan again. Her eyes wandered around and found Zila's green ones.

What are you planning? Kyla thought, staring intensely at the girl as if that way she could figure out what was coming.

"Miss Whixx. What are you doing?" Kyla blinked and found Mr Butland standing in front of her, eyebrows curved inwards. "Are you listening?"

"Of course." Kyla answered immediately as a reflex. She was always listening in lessons.

"What was I saying?"

"You were rambling about your time in the war." She replied. "Again."

Mr Butland gave her a hurtful look and Kyla smiled an apologetic smile. But the truth was that he did ramble on forever! Of course nobody ever listened to his stories anyway, no matter how many times he told them. Thankfully they were dismissed and so they made their way to the field where the festival was being held later today. It was mostly deserted, which was perfect because they still needed to drop the fake key.

"Quick." Mackenzie ordered and everyone picked up their pace.

They rushed towards the forest side of the yard and entered it. Kyla had never been inside the forest before and she had to say that it gave her chills with the dark shapes of trees looming over them, probably housing all kinds of horrible creatures. She gulped and moved closer to the figure on her right, which happened to be Kalen, who was also looking around, panicked.

"Are you ok?" Kyla asked.

"Dark." He whispered. "Very dark."

"It's ok." Mackenzie whispered from behind them, making Kyla jump and Kalen scream.

"Shhh." She slapped Kalen on the shoulder. "I already planted the key in its place. Time for the last step of our plan."

"May…Maybe we could…um…talk outside?" Daniel's shivering voice said.

"You are all so pathetic." Mackenzie observed but then she followed them out of the forest into the brightness of the festival, which was about to start. How long had they been in the forest?

"Daniel, don't move. There's a spider on your back." Kyla

said and of course her brother ran in a panic, shouting and screaming and flailing about.

"Is it gone?" He kept shouting but the spider clung on. Kyla grabbed Daniel by the arm to get him to stand still. She reached for the miniscule spider on his right arm and held it with cupped hands as she went towards the forest ground and dropped it lightly on the grass. When she turned back she saw Mackenzie on the ground roaring with laughter.

"YOU'RE SCARED OF SPIDERS? SPIDERS?"

"I think maybe we should go change and get our transfiddlers." Kalen looked at Kyla and she nodded, yanking Mackenzie's arm and dragging her away with her.

They swiped the card and went inside their dorm. Kyla hurried to her room to shower and put on her black shapeshifting suit, the one with the red dragon pouch and which now had the Optimistic Octopuses logo on the shoulder sleeve. She had forgotten how light and comfortable it was. Just like most things in Ocelia the suit could shapeshift. Something Kyla had discovered only recently and so now she changed the jump suit into looking like her everyday clothes so as to not arouse suspicion from Zila.

She made her way to the field and saw her friends in their own shapeshifting suits. Kyla whispered for them to change the look of it and in no time the four of them looked exactly the same as before. Together they walked casually, until they noticed Zila with her little group, sitting at the furthest corner of the canteen. Kyla moved closer to the group and raised her voice so that the group could hear them.

"I can't believe they have put the key to the artefacts room in the middle of the forest." she began, making sure that Zila could definitely overhear them. She watched as Zila stiffened and kept talking. "I mean anyone could steal it, it's been left totally unprotected, next to the tallest tree there." she continued.

She rounded the corner then transformed into a mouse and scurried underneath the table. Zila said an excuse and got up from the table quickly making her way across the hall. Kyla smiled, she had taken the bait. The plan was in motion.

Kyla chased after and looked as a falcon flew overhead. Daniel. Zila continued making her way past the hoard of people celebrating slinking past everyone like a panther. She whipped her head in every direction, probably checking to see if anyone was following her. Of course she didn't realise that the tiny mouse next to her was actually spying on her every move.

Zila took one final look and then she turned hurriedly and

ran into the forest, transforming into a snake that slithered over the soft grass. Kyla followed very closely behind. She turned the same way that Zila turned and copied her every move until Zila finally stopped in front of the most massive tree. And resting on its bark was the key.

The fake key.

It all came down to this…

Zila transformed back into herself and reached down for it, hand outstretched.

That's when the first plant shot out of the soil.

It launched itself through the soil like a rocket, pummelling against Zila's left arm and wrapping itself around her so tight that it looked painful. Then another vine joined in, taking Zila's legs and raising her off the ground as she gave a startled shriek. In a matter of seconds her body was covered with the thick arms that had grabbed her.

"We have you now!" Daniel screamed, jumping in front of her and standing triumphantly. Zila stared at him angrily.

"Get me out of here you twerp!" she shouted, her eyes furious. She continued struggling, cursing as she did.

"It's no use" Kalen said as he ran up beside the twins, Mackenzie, Zilef and Ingrid close behind. "We know you're the mole," he continued.

"A mole? You idiots, I'm not the mole." she insisted, her face almost completely covered by vines.

"Then how did you know about my mum?" Kyla responded, staring at the only eye she could see.

"Because my parents work as part of the team in charge of the search party. I'm not the mole I swear." she gasped for air.

"Fine." Daniel said. "Prove it!"

"Grab my left arm." She gasped. "Look at my wristband."

Kyla did as Zila asked and she stepped forward, slicing the vines from Zila's left arm with her transfiddler which was now a sword. She swiped the screen up and there on her messages was an emergency chat for a search party. On her band a logo gleamed in the moonlight. A logo of the search team, Mackenzie confirmed it. It was of the same model as one of her father's.

"See?" Zila coughed. "Can you get me out now?"

"First answer this!" Kalen spoke, stalking towards her. "If you're not the mole then why are you here?"

"What?"

"Why are you going after the artefacts key?" He was really close now right in front of her face, glaring at her.

"I knew about a mole ok?" She shouted. The vines were

now wrapping themselves across her mouth and Kyla could see her struggling harder. "I overheard the teachers talking about it after detention. They say some things go missing and I thought that if there truly was a mole then they would definitely come for the key."

"You really expect us to believe you?" Mackenzie growled.

"If…If I was…the mole…" Zila started, choking on the words, out of breath from the tight squeezing of the plants. "Wouldn't I have…a…a weapon on me?"

"I believe her." Kyla spoke up after a moment of silence.

"You do?" Everyone asked simultaneously.

"Yes I do." She stepped forward and sliced the plants off of the poor girl, who collapsed onto the ground and started gasping for air. Inhaling and exhaling. Inhaling and exhaling. She looked at the six people in front of her.

"Geez guys, next time do more research!" she replied annoyed. Zilef helped her up and looked apologetic.

"Sorry," he mumbled. Daniel meanwhile stepped ahead of them spreading his hands around.

"Hold on, if you're not the mole then that means that they're plan is still going to happen!" he explained anxiously. They all looked at each other, their eyes wide and the fear evident in them. "Quick you guys warn the teachers while

Kyla, Kalen, Mackenzie and I will look around for them." he said rapidly, not wasting a moment before jumping into action. Mackenzie, to no one's surprise, ran after him with Kalen and Kyla bringing up the rear.

"So what's the game plan?" Kalen asked panting.

"We find the real mole," Mackenzie explained. "Wait, stop" she whispered, grabbing and pulling them back.

"Wha-?" Kalen asked before looking at where Mackenzie was pointing.

Kyla squinted and could make out a dark hooded figure crouching near another patch of grass. Daniel sneaked towards them but the masked intruder must have heard him because they ran off leaving the four of them chasing after them.

"That's our mole," Daniel shouted excitedly.

"Wow really I wouldn't have guessed." Mackenzie said sarcastically. "Was it the hood or the fact that they're fleeing from us that gave them away?"

"I think we're gaini-"Kyla began before her foot got caught on a root and she went crashing into Mackenize. She pitched forward and lay on the ground, clutching her ankle in pain, as hot throbbing pains shot up her body.

"Owww." she gasped, tears leaking from her eyes. The

pain was almost unbearable.

"Don't move, I think you twisted it," Kalen said anxiously. "You guys go on ahead, I'll take care of her," he said. Daniel and Mackenzie looked at her, torn, and unsure of what to do.

"Go. You need to! You're the best fighters! I'll be fine," Kyla insisted. They nodded and sped off.

She groaned in pain and looked up at Kalen.

They were all alone in the darkness, while the mole was getting away….

# CHAPTER 19

## DANIEL

From the corner of his eye, Daniel could see Mackenzie right behind him, both of them running at their fullest. The shadow they were chasing was getting away very quickly and not even when Daniel transformed into a cheetah could he catch up. Now his side was hurting badly as he tried to breathe through the quick pace of their running. Mackenzie on the other hand was running at the exact same pace as when they had started. She had amazing stamina, unlike Daniel who really wanted to take a rest. The rain that was pouring on their faces also didn't help but Daniel couldn't do anything about that.

"They're getting away!" Mackenzie screamed and she picked up the pace leaving Daniel behind.

The mole however seemed to have heard her a second

later as there was the sound of a gunshot. Mackenzie jumped to the left, clutching Daniel's arm really hard and moving him with her.

"Watch out!" She screamed. "A bomb is coming towards us!"

"How do you know?"

BOOM!

The trees around them burst into flames causing them to stop and turn. Overhead lightning exploded onto the scene striking a different tree and causing it to collapse blocking the route the mole had taken. The fire quickly spread surrounding them and causing them to feel the intense heat being radiated. Daniel turned into a tiger, quickly looking for a way out then began to climb one of the few trees remaining. The rain continued to crash onto him as he stood on a branch and began to run. He leaped off and over the roaring flames, as lightning struck behind him. He landed on the ground and let out a roar before Mackenzie landed beside him. He saw her nod and the two once again set off, their paws leaping simultaneously off the floor.

The shadowy figure had returned. It was right in front of them, mere metres in front. It turned, its black mask glinting in the eerie glow of moonlight. A small square was being held in his left hand and it transformed into a scythe, with an extremely sharp end. Daniel flinched for a second but then transformed back to human form and took out his own transfiddler, which transformed into two swords. Mackenzie clutched a double-bladed sword beside him and the two of them faced the figure.

"Who are you?" Daniel screamed.

There was no response.

"Who ARE YOU?" Mackenzie exclaimed.

She lunged, twirling her double-bladed sword and striking at the villain. She skidded to the right just in time to avoid the sharp end of the scythe and did a backwards flip onto a small hilltop. Her anger pushed her forward at such a high velocity that she collided with the figure, rolling around in the dirt and hitting them over and over again but the figure threw her away from them brutally. Luckily, Mackenzie was great at combat and she landed on both her feet, rushing forward again and hitting the figure once more.

All this took a matter of seconds and Daniel felt useless during it but soon he got a good grip on his sword and he sprung towards the fight. The mole sensed his arrival and dodged the attack leaping over the sword with expert grace. Daniel swung his swords and they crashed against the mole's own weapon, sparks leaping through the air, the raindrops splattered onto their skin. Daniel growled then pushed onto the attacker launching attacks onto them until they were pushed back onto the tree behind them.

"Yield," Daniel said furiously, forcing the blades against their scythe. The mole kicked him then ducked under his weapons before cartwheeling back into a defensive stance. Mackenzie shrieked and leaped at him while Daniel charged him, his swords glinting against the moonlight overhead. The mole danced like a ballerina dodging and striking against their blows before landing against one of the rocky walls. The scythe hummed before being replaced by a nun chuck with a curved hilt. The masked traitor swung it in a fluid and graceful movement causing the wall to tremble and large boulders to collapse and fall towards Daniel. He gasped and flung himself to the side but the boulders overwhelmed him and he was soon covered in them and unable to move. Daniel pushed and grunted but they would not move.

"Mackenzie? Are you there?!" he asked, his voice slicing through the quiet.

"I'm pinned. I can't move" came the reply. Daniel struggled and squirmed under the pressure. The claustrophobia was beginning to sink in. He started hyperventilating as he pounded and punched the boulders. But to no avail. He stopped and sat down breathing in deeply and trying to concentrate. In his head he heard his mom, sister and friends all crying for help. He knew that they needed him. He opened his eyes and saw that he was now looming over the rocks looking down on them. He had transformed into something. But what? He didn't have a chance to find out as he returned to normal.

"Mackenzie, where are you?" he screamed as he turned around to look for her. The darkness made it difficult to see even with the moon over them and the rain hurt his visibility further making it almost impossible to see anything.

"Over here." A hand rose through a set of boulders near him and Daniel grabbed it pulling his friend out from under the rubble and into a relief filled hug.

"Yeah yeah I know, I'm happy to see you too." Mackenzie grumbled. She pushed him away and stood up, her cheeks slightly red most likely from the strain. "Come on we've got a traitor to catch," she said before running into the opening of a cave.

Daniel smiled and chased after her making sure to go as slowly as possible. He caught up to her as she listened in from a corner. He turned and his jaw fell in astonishment. There was a secret garden in the cave.

"How?" he whispered dumbfounded.

"I don't know" Mackenzie replied equally stunned before silently making her way through the area. Daniel ran a hand over the smooth walls, which didn't suit the cave at all.

"This isn't a cave. It's the mole's layer of operations!" he breathed before moving to where Mackenzie stood hunched over a computer and set of books.

"Look!" she said, pointing at the books in front of her. "It's the missing ones from the library and there's a gardening one as well." Daniel picked one up and to his surprise it transformed into a falcon book. Daniel frowned as a distant memory tugged at his brain.

Where had he seen that book before?

He didn't have a moment to dwell on it as Mackenzie tackled him just as the mole entered the room. Daniel watched as it called a drone to their hand and entered two small red vials into its sockets.

"Yes master, the plan is almost ready." they said, their dark, distorted and heavy voice resonating through the chamber. Daniel continued to think. He knew that he was missing something, there was something too familiar about this.

"Soon you will rise again and Ocelia will be yours to rule at last" they proclaimed before the drone flew off. It was here that Daniel and Mackenzie couldn't take it any longer. Mackenzie nodded and grabbed onto the ceiling using special gloves Daniel had invented before swinging over to the villain and kicking them in the gut. The mole gasped and swung at her before Daniel leaped at him, his swords crashing against the mask that concealed their identity. The mask snapped and fell to the ground in pieces as the antagonist flew across the room, before landing in a corner. Daniel ran to Mackenzie before helping her up. Together they made their way to the fallen villain who was laughing and wheezing.

"You fools!" the voice began, the distortion flickering in every two words, "It's over! You've failed." Daniel squinted at the figure, the voice sounding very familiar to someone close to him.

"Who are you?" he asked, drawing his sword against their neck.

"You don't want to know." was the reply.

"Turn" Daniel said gravely, his voice dripping with venom as slowly the figure turned and looked into Daniel's eyes, the rest of the mask and hood falling to the ground.

Daniel gasped and behind him Mackenzie took a step

back, stunned.

"It can't be-" he said…

The mole was…

# CHAPTER 20

# KYLA

"OW!"

Kyla swatted Kalen's hand away from her ankle as he reached for it again. She had honestly never been in such pain. Her eyes were shut tightly, not wanting to see the position of her foot and how swollen it looked.

"Sorry. I need to see your ankle." Kyla felt a soft hand grab her leg and she opened her eyes, looking at Kalen as he examined her ankle.

"Wow. It's really bad." Kalen mumbled.

"Thanks!"

"I need to get some branches to build some support for it. I'll be back."

Kyla watched him leave, shivering in the cold night. It was very dark now, almost pitch black and Kyla could hear the scattering of animals near her but she was too afraid to look. She didn't want to see the millions of spiders crawling around the branch she was sitting on. Unfortunately, dangerous animals appeared to be the least of her problems at the moment. She took a deep breath and willed herself to look down at her ankle.

She could no longer see it. All she saw was a humongous red lump wrapped around where her ankle had been ten minutes ago.

She looked back up, ordering herself not to cry. It didn't hurt that much. It just hurt a lot. Rustling sounds came from behind her and Kalen came running towards her.

"Ok. Sit still for a second." He said, whilst pulling out the branches and leaves that he had collected in the forest. He knelt down and started pulling the leaves and branches around Kyla's ankle.

"That should keep some pressure off it but you can't walk much." Kalen sat next to Kyla.

"I need to help Daniel! He could be in danger!"

"He's smart. He'll be fine." Kalen reassured her but Kyla wasn't so sure. They were completely in the dark. The mole wasn't who they thought it was and now Daniel and Mackenzie were chasing after this dangerous traitor.

"The best thing we can do is bring you back to the dorms and find some medical support." Kalen looked her in the eyes waiting for an answer and she reluctantly nodded. He helped her up and together they began to walk to the school. The rain had begun to pour heavily hindering their ability to see but they trudged on for several miles. Kyla hadn't realised how far into the forest they had actually gone.

A throbbing pain raced up Kyla's ankle and she gave a yelp.

"Are you ok?" Kalen grabbed her by both arms.

"It hurts. Can we rest?"

"Of course." Kalen led Kyla over to an unusually large bush and sat her down. He, meanwhile, said that there were these berries that might help release the pain and so he stuck his head into the bush.

Kyla froze.

Right in front of her, slithering towards them, was the biggest snake she had ever seen. It had fangs the size of her thigh and the body so thick that it made the branch she was sitting on earlier look small. It slithered up to them, its tongue flickering in and out around its long-curved fangs. Its blood-red eyes fixed themselves upon Kyla and Kalen and it slowly began to circle them. Blood dripped from its venomous fangs as overhead lightning struck, illuminating its black, striped body.

"Kalen?" Kyla's voice wobbled.

"What is it?"

"Huge snake!"

"WHAT?"

He popped his head out of the bush and looked in its direction. His eyes widened with fear.

"Run through the bush!" He yelled as he helped Kyla up.

"There could be more in the bush!"

"I just checked! There's absolutely nothing in that bush!" Kyla got pushed into the bush and she fell hard on something. Something metallic.

Metallic?

The floor below her vanished and she fell and fell and fell until her body hit another, harder floor. Groaning with even more pain, she rubbed her head and looked around. Concrete walls surrounded her and she appeared to be in a room. She glanced to her left and saw a keyboard. She went up to it and tapped one of the keys. A large screen flickered to life and Kyla realised it needed a password. She got to work on disabling the wires to get past it and within minutes the screen whirred to life and Kyla was in. She watched as the entire place lit up and she found herself looking at a long narrow hallway filled with incubators, eggs and test tubes.

A yell sounded from beside her and Kalen fell. She helped him up as he clutched his back in pain. Kyla grabbed onto Kalen to remain upright and together they explored the hidden laboratory.

"Look at this stuff," Kalen said, pointing at all the incubators. "It's like they were making something". He went up to one of the long cylinders and began typing on the keyboard before a loud alarm began to wail, turning the room bright red.

"Intruders!" it repeated. Kyla covered her ears as the deafening noise invaded her ears. She felt Kalen's hand grab her wrist and he began to pull her away.

"C'mon this place is about to self-destruct." he cried urgently.

"But the evidence- the plans" she exclaimed worriedly.

"There's no time- GET DOWN!" he shouted, tackling her to the ground just as the place exploded pushing them further down the hall as everything erupted in a ball of fire. Kyla got up groggily, clutching her head.

"Let's keep moving." Kalen told her panting and they set off again through the dark maze of corridors until they reached a large doorway. Kalen quickly transformed into an elephant and broke it down before pulling Kyla in with him. However as the lights switched on Kyla found herself flabbergasted and in shock, because lying on one of the tables strapped and chained to it was…

Her mother.

Kyla screamed in joy and hobbled over to her as fast as possible. Her mother looked awful, bruises and cuts marred her body which was littered in scars. She had a swollen lip and a black eye but Klya had never been happier to see her.

"Mom , wake up, it's me, we've come to rescue you" she exclaimed, desperately trying to rouse her.

"Kyla?" she whispered, her eyes flickering open. Tears of joy escaped her and soon Kyla was clinging to her in a warm, relief filled embrace.

"Kyla, listen to me." the mom said gravely "You are in great danger we need to-"

"We know," Kyla replied, cutting her off. "However, what we don't know is who the mole is. Who is it mom? Who trapped you here?"

Her mom took a deep breathe before looking at her eyes and whispering:

"It's-"…

# CHAPTER 21

## DANIEL

"DELVIN?" he and Mackenzie asked together, both equally as stunned as the other.

How could it have been Delvin?  It was impossible yet as Daniel thought harder it made sense.

"Surprise!" Delvin replied sarcastically, making small jazz hands. He smirked and his unusually dark eyes glinted maliciously.

"How?" Daniel asked, still reeling from the shock.

"Really I'm surprised you couldn't figure it out earlier, it was so obvious!" he laughed. Daniel put the sword closer to his neck.

"Explain everything, what are you doing?" he growled. "Why did you come to this school in the first place?"

"Huh. As if I'd tell you!"

Mackenzie inched forward, the tip of her bladed sword dangerously near Delvin's face. "Tell us." She said in a low threatening voice. Sweat dripped from her face, which was still a deathly pale colour caused by the betrayal. Delvin snorted in disbelief, his smirk widening.

"Oh please you don't have the guts to kill me!" Delvin sneered a sharp glint in his eye. He adjusted his position calmly and smiled at them untroubled.

"Try me." Mackenzie growled her sword pressing against his throat, her eyes steely and furious. Daniel took a step back, surprised at her tone. Delvin must have noticed it too because his smile lessened as if he realised she was capable of doing it.

"Fine, I'll talk!" he spat, glaring at both of them. "Our plan from the beginning was to bring you both out of hiding and into Ocelia. Carefully planted spies alerted us of your whereabouts and so we moved in to apprehend you. We would have too if Icarus had not been there. That messed up our plan slightly." he began stepping slightly back to try and get out of Mackenzie's reach but she pressed the tip harder against his throat.

"So we had to improvise. I was sent to school to keep an eye on you and complete my other mission of course." he continued his voice lowering as his chin began to bleed due to the blade tip scratching at it.

"To assassinate the leaders of the kingdoms." Daniel finished. Delvin barked a laugh.

"How stupid are you? We never wanted to kill the leaders. We have moles in every layer of society capable of killing them at a moment's notice. No, our plan revolves around those flowers in my garden," he started, pointing to where they were.

"I don't believe you," Daniel threatened.

"I swear. Those plants are the moonstone herbs that's why the plan was scheduled for today. They only grow during the phase of the third moon rising because they need the special light radiated from the moon to photosynthesise."

"Why do it at school then? What was the point of that?" Mackenzie pressed.

"The school's soil has a special type of protein which makes it the only place capable of growing the moonstone. That's why this school has specialised greenhouses so that they can grow these kinds of flowers. In fact, it's the only place on Ocelia that grows them as it's considered the safest and therefore least likely to be broken into." he continued, sweat beginning to drip down his forehead.

"Why do you need the moonstone?" Daniel continued.

"You know why. Once the plant photosynthesises it creates a sugar which has regenerative qualities capable of making anyone strong. Who wouldn't want that kind of power?"

"So that's your plan? To be the strongest person out there?"

"I have to say I really overestimated your detective abilities. Haven't you learnt yet? The power isn't for me. It never has been. It's for a greater purpose. Soon we will have an army and we'll destroy everyone in Ocelia." he laughed again, the cackle resonating around the room.

"Who's we?" Mackenzie glanced at Daniel, fear in her eyes.

Delvin roared with laughter. "You'll see!"

With that, a sort of black energy sprouted from inside of him, enveloping him in darkness and transforming him into an enormous dragon with wings a hundred feet wide and teeth the size of Daniel's sword. It roared and from its mouth came a burning hot flame.

Mackenzie launched herself at Daniel as another flame erupted in their direction.

"Do something!" She screamed. Her eyes turned a deep purple and she shrunk into the shape of a panther, springing onto the dragon's wings and clawing at them. Daniel knew that they stood no chance now but he changed into a lion and raced to assist Mackenzie.

Delvin was swatting at Mackenzie now, bursting flame after flame and trying to shake her off. His nostrils filled with flames from frustration and Daniel looked, helplessly, as the dragon's claws grabbed Mackenzie and catapulted her across the forest. She transformed back and hit a tree bark, collapsing to the ground.

"MACKENZIE!"

Daniel raced over to her crumpled form. Her head was swollen and blood was falling from her mouth. Anger boiled inside of Daniel. His whole body vibrated with it. His whole body vibrated with drive.

Vibrated with power.

He screamed and his power grew stronger and stronger.

He looked down at Delvin.

Down?

Daniel looked over himself and realised he was a dragon as well! He saw large red and green wings protruding from his back and his tail was a long, elegant thing, with a ball of spikes at the end of it. Daniel roared and flames erupted from his mouth.

"Impossible!" screamed Delvin, still in shock. Daniel

tackled him, grabbing his long, thick neck and smashing it into the ground before breathing bolts of lightning onto his face. Delvin wailed in agony but with a sharp scratch at Daniel's underbelly, he freed himself and breathed fiery flames upon his enemy. Daniel pushed through them digging his claws into Delvin's face before clawing at his wings. Delvin cried in alarm then crashed to the ground shooting fireballs all over the place, but Daniel dodged them and launched himself into the air, his new, powerful wings supporting him as he flew overhead sending fire and lightning upon Delvin.

Ok time to be spontaneous. Daniel thought to himself before turning and diving at Delvin, breathing fire as he spun creating a miniature fire tornado which surrounded his body. The move left Delvin dumbstruck and with one final swift attack Daniel grabbed his neck and subdued him.

"Transform back!" Daniel growled, placing the sharpest of his nails on Delvin's neck. Delvin gulped and changed into his human form but now he had the same dark energy surrounding him.

"Don't try to escape!" Daniel warned and he set his feet on the ground and scooped up Mackenzie.

"You'll regret this, you will suffer when we rise. You'll see.

He will rise and when he does you will never escape with your life. "

"Ocelia is doomed!".

# CHAPTER 22

# KYLA

Kyla opened her eyes groggily before sitting up in her hospital cot. Where was she? The last thing she remembered was the teachers arriving and helping her into a stretcher. She looked around the barren room littered with hospital beds and made the assumption that she was in the infirmary. She turned to her right and saw her friends in similar beds though they seemed to be more awake than her.

"About time you woke up!" Mackenzie exclaimed excitedly, her head in a bandage and her face covered in smaller band aids.

"What happened?" Kyla replied.

"You've been unconscious for 2 days" Daniel answered, his arm in a sling and a long scar over his right eye.

2 days? She'd figured that she had been sleeping for a while

but she hadn't imagined that it would have been that long. Her stomach grumbled softly and she looked around trying to shake off the sleep.

"What happened?" she asked, rubbing her head which was in a lot of pain.

"Must've been exhausted. I mean all you had was a broken bone." Mackenzie scoffed. "I had a broken arm and a concussion but was I asleep for 2 days? Nope, I was only unconscious for ten hours. How embarrassing."

Kalen snorted. "That's nothing? I had nothing. I had a broken pinky. Pinky!" he said.

"Ladies and gentlemen we have a winner," Daniel said sarcastically before throwing some candy into his mouth.

"Have the teachers asked us about what happened?" Kyla asked, concerned before grabbing some chocolate nesting on her bedside table. What if she had been asleep for the interrogations? She sighed and began opening the wrapper.

"Not really," Kalen replied. "My mom has been waiting for you to be awake before getting the full story but she does know that Delvin is the mole."

It was then that the doors opened and the teachers strode in. Ms Smith led the way with Mr Smithy, Ms Orgi and Mr Butland close behind. They were all deadly serious except for

Mr Smithy who appeared to be drooling over a chocolate bar.

Ms Smith paused in front of Kyla. "Tell us everything!"

Together the 4 friends explained the series of events and after around 20 minutes the teachers were left stunned. Mr Smithy looked a bit dazed, staring at his chocolate until it started to melt on his hand.

"Thank you for telling us this," Ms Smith said after a long pause. "We are grateful for what you did and impressed by your efforts." Behind her Mr Smithy snorted in disgust. The adults wished them a speedy recovery before leaving the room. Except for Ms Smith who stayed behind.

"Hey guys, listen, I know you've been through a lot and you're tired but Delvin is refusing to speak in prison unless you talk to him." she told them looking at their eyes. "I understand if you don't want to or if you're not ready but I want you to consider talking to him."

"When?" asked Daniel curiously.

"Whenever you want," Ms Smith replied.

"Ok let's do it right now!"

***

The four of them were led down a dark narrow passageway

by a bulky guard. He had several scars lining his muscular arms and a black tattoo of a skull over his left eyebrow.

"Stay off the walls, they're electrified." he warned them darkly, moving Kalen further away from the doors. "You lay a finger on them and you'll wake up dazed in 3 weeks and numb all over."

The entire place gave Kyla the creeps. It was eerie and plain and quite frankly she didn't understand why the academy even kept this prison on site. It did not fit with the glamorous white classrooms.

"How much further?" Kalen asked, exhausted, voicing Kyla's own complaints.

"Quit whining! We're here." the guard replied crossly before leading them to a set of chairs in front of a steel gate. He stepped behind them then lifted the gate to reveal someone sat smugly in a chair and smiling.

Delvin.

"Well, well, well, look who became popular all of a sudden" he started before letting out a cackle. "To what do I owe this pleasure?"

"You asked for us, Delvin." Kyla snapped her hands becoming fists by her sides. Delvin sat up, his chained hands coming to a rest on his table.

"So I did." he said, his lip curling cruelly into a sneer. "You know this is only temporary right?" he spoke confidently, walking across his barren cell. "Soon I'll be free and you will all suffer!"

"Oh wow look at that, the villain is trying to scare us by ranting about his failed plan. Is that why we're here? To hear you threaten us?" Daniel asked cooly.

"No. The reason I asked you to come is because I want to make a deal. I can help you, you know." he explained. His voice had a hint of excitement that made Kyla's hairs stand on end and his smirk made something inside of her boil. He had tricked them all once before. Never again!

"What would a trapped convict have that we'd need?" Mackenzie replied coldly, her eyes as cold as ice.

For the first time in their visit Delvin's smug demeanour faded, giving Kyla a glimpse of his angry, resentful side.

"How about we each ask a question? I'll answer truthfully if you do?" Delvin asked his hands now behind his head while he leaned back.

"I don't like this." Kalen whispered to Kyla and she nodded in agreement.

"Yeah but we don't have a choice." she argued before turning to Delvin. "You have a deal."

"Perfect," he replied, his eyes glinting dangerously. "I'll go first. How much do you trust the people around you?" he began his hands coming to a rest in front of him.

"Why?" Kyla inquired.

"I'm the one asking the questions here." he replied angrily.

"Ok fine. I trust them fully" Daniel cut in glaring at Delvin. Delvin's smile broadened and he began to tap his fingers thoughtfully on the table making a pattern which Kyla recognised was morse code for stupid.

"Now it's our turn. Who do you work for?" Kyla pressed leaning forward. Delvin's mouth curved into a malicious smile.

"A higher power. Someone who very soon will rise again." he told them.

"That's not an answer," Daniel snapped coldly.

"It is, just not the one you wanted to hear." Delvin replied, his broad smile opening, showing his teeth.

"We foiled your plan here didn't we? And now that we know you're a mole you'll never be able to pull something like that again." Kalen explained confidently but Delvin just burst out laughing, his cackles filling the room.

"Is that what you really believe?" he questioned, laughing even harder when they nodded.

"Do you really think this is over? What happened the other day was just one plan, a fluke. The people I work for have hundreds of backup plans just waiting to be set up. Just like I am not the only mole in the government. The government is filled with walking lies. You think the people around you are trustworthy? You'll see. Everything Ocelia was built on was a lie. Our entire history is a lie, but it's all covered up. Kept silent and invisible from our history by our leaders. But why? That's the question. But soon, very soon, these lies will be exposed and the entire world will see the world through our eyes. They'll see a government no longer shielded by corruption and lies, but instead the utter trainwreck that they are." He recounted. Kyla looked at her friends and saw their faces dominated by shock and fear.

"I can tell you're surprised." Delvin continued. "I told you already that he will rise and when he does our armies will lay waste to this kingdom and anyone who gets in our way. It's just a matter of time until I'm free and when I am you won't live to see the light of day again. My bosses want you to join us but I know you're far too dangerous. I should have killed you when I had the chance!" he finished threateningly.

He leaped up and punched the wall as hard as he could. Kyla screamed and fell back in her chair while Kalen jumped in surprise. Delvin cackled with glee, his nails continuing to scratch the window, his hands punching the wall, getting bloodier with each hit. His face had left all reason, his eyes turned to slits and blood dripped from his hands. He pressed his head against the glass, forcing them to see his crazed state, dishevelled hair and faraway eyes. The guards rushed into the room and ushered them out but not before Kyla heard Delvin's final threat.

"This isn't over, we will have our revenge and you will pay. I swear to that. I SWEAR!"...

# CHAPTER 23

# DANIEL

School life continued as normal, however after the recent events classes just weren't that interesting. With only 4 weeks remaining of school Daniel still had his finals to prepare for and the final game in the Changeball Cup. Decker was in a frenzy furiously berating his players, including today just minutes before the game leaving the team incredibly annoyed and mutinous.

"Why can't he just leave?" asked Ashlin. The rest of the team looked just as angry as her, though with her blonde pixie cut and maroon streaks she looked extra annoyed.

"Maybe he's just stressed at the fact that we can finally win the cup!" Skylor replied, pushing her brown hair out of her angry face. Her fringe kept getting in her face, which was why she was in the middle of getting a head band the same colour as her streaks; blue. Those electric blue eyes of hers buzzed with excitement.

The rest of the assembled team mumbled in agreement though they were not excited like her. They were all still too busy fuming at their couch's horrible behaviour.

"I know the final is in a couple of minutes but the guy has got to chill. There's no way we'll perform well if he talks to us like that." Trayton chipped in, his identical twin brother Zim nodded in agreement. Daniel enjoyed having them on the team, partly because it was as if they had one brain but also because they always lightened the mood. Mackenzie meanwhile was mumbling something under her breath which, if a teacher overheard would have landed her a couple weeks of detention.

"Come on guys, let's just ignore him and relax," Daniel said. "If we just block him out we'll be fine". Zim snorted behind him.

"Yeah right. I swear the guy has issues!" Kalen agreed before Roxy barged into the room holding a clipboard in her hand.

"Ok guys this is it! The final game!" she began, waving the clipboard in the direction of Daniel's face. It missed him by mere metres.

Mackenzie, fearing a quick speech, cut her off.

"Yeah yeah we get it, work together and all that mumbo jumbo." Mackenzie grumbled before beginning to head out the changing room.

"Go octopuses!" she shouted leading to a chorus of "Go Octopuses" from the others. Daniel heard the roar of the crowd before he saw it as Mackenzie led the team onto the pitch. They needed to win or else they would lose the cup. Daniel took his position in goal then watched as Mackenzie shook hands with the crocodile's captain. He looked around and saw the large mass of green crocodiles which had assembled roaring to their heart's content. Out of the corner of his eyes he saw Ingrid commentating though he could only hear Malcom's commentary slamming them. He looked on and waited for the whistle, then the game began.

The crocodiles began the attack though Daniel wasn't worried as his defence was incredibly good though he couldn't believe his eyes as Zila got past all the players including Skylar leaving her one on one against Daniel. He rushed out and barely managed to parry the ball out of play.

What was happening? He thought to himself a minute later as the crocodiles once again almost took the lead however Skylor tracked back and cleared it off the line.

"Wake up!" He screamed exasperated but they didn't, leaving him stranded as he could only watch in horror as Kalen took out Zila giving away a penalty. Daniel bounced on the goal line before diving to his right and making the save; however he watched as the ball looped over him and into the back of the net. The green section of the crowd roared in ecstasy.

"And it's one nil to the crocodile's after an awful start to the game by the octopuses Daniel fumbles his penalty save and allows the opposition to score. What a bunch of losers!" Malcom was saying though Daniel could barely hear it over the sound of boos being thrown his way. He knew they were in trouble especially with Ingrid being so quiet.

His thoughts were proven right as the Octopuses entered half time 3-0 down and shocked into silence. He sat down next to Trayton and saw his green eyes filled with tears, while on his other side Zim's black and yellow hair was pulled over his downcast gaze. They sat in silence, all of them shocked and distraught. The silence was only broken by Mackenzie getting up and standing in the middle of the room.

"What just happened?" she began. "That was one of the worst halves I have ever seen and I've seen a lot!" they all looked down in shame, her words stinging them and cutting deep.

"You know what the problem is?" she continued looking each of them in the eye as she did. "We're not playing like a team. It's that simple. We have to start communicating and talking because I believe in all of you." She paused to let that sink in. "Except for you Kalen."

"Hey!" he cried. However, that broke the tension leading to everyone breaking out in laughter. Kyla bumped Mackenzie's shoulder as they both shared a laugh over Kalen's face of shock.

"Alright, let's do this thing." Their captain said before once again leading them out of the tunnel. Daniel took one last look around then breathed in once, a deep, nervous breath and followed her out of the room and into the blinding light.

***

"And it's a goal for the Octopuses!" Ingrid was shouting while Daniel punched the air in the goal. Daniel couldn't believe the comeback his teammates were doing. With only minutes to go they were now 3-3.

"What do you make of their performance Malcom?" she asked and Daniel saw her huge smile on the big screen that was broadcasting the game.

"It's a fluke! Even with those wings, Kyla should never have gotten past those defenders! It's absolutely shocking!" he replied disgustedly as the Octopus crowd, which had been quiet for the majority of the game, roared like the ocean during a tropical storm. Daniel looked at the clock.

5 minutes.

That's it. Just one more goal…

But the dream was shattered when Zila dived in the box, her wings crumbling and appealing for a penalty. He couldn't believe it. What a cheater he thought to himself. Daniel went up to her and looked her in the eyes confidently before mimicking what Mackenzie had done to Zilef earlier that year and whispering a threat to her. Zila looked rattled. Daniel looked at the clock again.

3 minutes. He needed to save this or they would lose. But if he did save it, then maybe, just maybe, they could get another one. He waited for the whistle.

Then he heard it and dived at full stretch with his fingers grazing the ball…

And saving it. He got up and saved the rebound with his legs, grabbed the ball with his massive tentacles and spotting Kyla on the opposite end of the pitch, he threw the ball at her then looked at the clock nervously.

1 minute.

Kyla was flying. He watched as she dodged under the defender's outstretched legs and arms.

He watched as she passed it to where Mackenzie was unmarked.

He watched as Mackenzie leaped into the air and scored the winning goal.

The next 30 seconds were a blur. All he remembered was running the length of the pitch where the rest of the team had dogpiled their captain who was screaming at the bottom of it, what sounded a lot like "Get off me!" though no one seemed to hear it as the referee blew her whistle and the stadium erupted. Daniel looked up and saw his friends charging onto the pitch, Zilef being the first to reach him and tackling him to the ground before he was pulled into a hug by Gabbi. He stepped back still grabbing onto Zilef and Gabbi in time to see Mackenzie being lifted into the air by the team.

Kyla raced towards Daniel, grabbing him by the ear.

"You did it!" She screamed. "You DID IT!" She yelled before turning around and hugging the rest of the team. He could see the crocodiles slumped on the floor, broken, as their win had been snatched in a spectacular comeback. He watched proudly as a beaming Rhea passed the trophy to him before it was stolen from his grasp by Mackenzie, who lifted it up to the cheers of the crowd. Then, the celebrations really began.

***

Daniel stood at the front door of Woodford looking at his report card. He had managed straight As in every subject. Even from Mr Smithy though he had a sneaking suspicion that he only got it because Ms Smith had intervened. Pyro fidgeted around his legs, looking up at Daniel with a pitiful look before shrieking in fear and diving behind him.

"Hello there Mr Whixx." Daniel turned around to see the cause of the problem. Mr Smithy. The little man was perched on his scooter, staring right at him unblinkingly.

"Hello sir."

"Leaving so soon? And without saying goodbye to me?" he asked, his eyes glinting dangerously.

"Well you see our mom just got a new house and we haven't really had the chance to talk to her so I was kind of hoping to get out of here quickly." he explained leaving out the parts where he thought that the old man was insane, a maniac and senile.

"Before you go take this. A signed CD of my new Number 1. Hit song 'Who sucks? Mr Whixx!'" he told Daniel as he gave him a small CD. Daniel stared at him horrified before watching the old man zoom off on his annoying scooter. Oh how Daniel wished to puncture those tires.

He'd have to settle for burning the CD…

"Hey Daniel!" he heard before turning and seeing his friends Zilef, Ingrid and Gabbi all assembled behind him. He had made many friends. But he had also lost one.

"Keep in touch, hear?" Zilef told him, giving him a high five before picking up his stuff and making his way out of the academy. Daniel turned and slapped Lukas and Vazquez on the back before he turned and hugged Gabbi. He was about to do the same to Ingrid but was rudely interrupted by Mackenzie who had somehow managed to spawn there. She appeared annoyed at him though he didn't understand why.

Girls.

What was really strange was that Mackenzie smiled at Gabbi, who had come back to say goodbye to Kyla and Kalen. He watched Gabbi grab Kalen tightly before giving another hug to Kyla.

Kalen walked up to him as well, staring at the CD before

shaking his head and laughing to himself.

"Look after yourself." Kalen mumbled.

"You too." Daniel clapped him on the back. Kalen turned to Kyla and hugged her, wishing her a restful summer. He turned to Mackenzie and she yanked him by the shirt before threatening him menacingly. She said it so softly that Daniel could only catch snippets. But those words were enough to make him start drafting a speech for Kalen's eulogy.

Once everyone had gone, Mackenzie walked up and slapped Daniel on the arm.

"We will meet during the summer. Understand?" She told him with a smile. "We need to figure out our next few plans to land detention on the very first day back!"

Daniel laughed. "Obviously!" though he stopped when he noticed Kyla looking at him. She narrowed her eyes at him and Mackenzie. It's like she had a secret sense for when Daniel was planning some mischief. She did not approve of detention, which made getting it just that much better!

She walked over to him, with a purple transportation bubble in her right hand.

"Ready to go home? Ready to see mom?" She asked him and he grinned.

He looked to where he could make out his mom's outline

waving them over to their new home.

"Oh yeah!" he replied before grabbing his bags and pushing his sister out of the way. And with Pyro flying right next to him, he jumped through the portal, transporting himself to their new house and into their new life.

# EPILOGUE

The darkness engulfed the castle as overhead lightning and thunder crashed illuminating the barren land in an eerie glow. But deep within the castle, deep within the lair of evil, two people were talking.

Their plan had failed. That was true. But they would not stop. They had what they needed for the next phase. Their mole had not been a whole disaster.

"When will it be ready?" one figure asked her snide, cackly voice echoing through the empty castle.

"Soon." The other replied. She knew that the boy had given her the correct vials. The correct samples of DNA that were needed to create the monstrosity that they would use to make Woodford and Ocelia kneel before them.

"Very soon. Once it is awake it will lay waste to the SSSS and all of Ocelia. They will regret ever imprisoning us." they continued, their hood covering their dark, scarred face. "This monster will allow our master to rise again and when he does no one, not even those children will stand in our way."

However what they didn't know was that deep within the home, deep within the evil and lies, their experiment had worked. In the incubator was the next plan. The monster that would allow them to rise to the top. The beast that would help them capture the twins once and for all. It had never been about the mom.

It was always about the twins.

The great experiment, the new monster, opened its blood-red eyes for the first time and let out one single blood curdling scream as it thrashed and thought one thing.

KILL THE TWINS…

# ACKNOWLEDGEMENTS

This book would never have been possible without the incredible support of everyone in our lives. First, to our beautiful mom Nuria Lozano for giving us life and introducing us to reading. You sparked our passion and we are eternally grateful for everything you have done for us. When we had given up on reading, you persuaded us by buying every possible book and making us read them until we found one which we loved. Our love for reading is thanks to you and your hard work.

Next, a massive thank you to our dad Jorge Sanz for inspiring us to write our own book, after seeing the amazing work that was your own novel. On top of that you spent countless hours helping us with designing our beautiful front cover, which couldn't have looked better. Thank you for being the first to read this novel and for giving us your positive energy.

We would also like to give a giant thank you to our phenomenal older sister Lydia. Without your endless creative writing lessons, we would have never discovered our love and talent for writing. We love and appreciate everything you've done for us and for helping us grow and mature into the people we are today. It would never have been possible without your support and guidance.

Another huge thanks has to go to our friends for being the inspiration behind some of our characters (especially the villains). Your support has been immense and we would have never done it without you guys so thank you all so much.

Finally, thank you to our readers, yes YOU, because without you, this wouldn't be possible. Thank you for your patience with reading the book, and we really hope you guys enjoyed it. Can't wait to write the sequel!

# ABOUT THE AUTHORS

The authors Macarena and David Sanz Lozano are a pair of 17-year-old twins, who originate from Spain but have travelled around the globe and been fortunate enough to grow up in a variety of different countries.

With their passion for books as well as Drama, they channelled all their personality into these pages of their first-ever novel.

They adapted, enriched and translated the book "HAINDS and the quantum mind" from the original Spanish version to the English version.

The twins enjoy watching football and Marvel and are fervent admirers of both crime and fantasy novels alike. They hope to continue to develop their novel into a series 'Defenders of the Wild'.